Troubled Girls Find Love

THE COMPLETE COLLECTION

KATHRYN REIGN

KATHRYN REIGN PUBLISHING

Copyright

Troubled Girls Find Love
The Complete Collection

© Copyright 2023 Kathryn Reign

Cover Design by Les (germancreative)

Troubled Girls Find Love

Contents

In Love with my Best Friend

TROUBLED GIRLS FIND LOVE

In Love with my Best Friend

My name is Lauren.

I have a caring husband and two beautiful children.

But I can't stop thinking about... **Him**.

Ever since I found my old phone, I've been haunted by memories of Felix, bringing back feelings that I've tried so hard to ignore.

I feel guilty for regretting my marriage, for channeling the affection I should be having for my husband onto another man.

But I can no longer deny it.

I'm in love with my best friend.

A romance short story that features love, regret, and betrayal.

Chapter One

I wake up in my bedroom, staring up at the plain, white ceiling. Letting out a small sigh, I climb out of my comfy bed and head downstairs, my ears suddenly being greeted by the sound of my children.

"Good morning!" My husband gives me a small smile when I enter the living room. He's sitting on the couch, the children playing in front of him. "I have to work today. But I'll try to come home early and spend the evening with you."

Nodding, I take a seat beside him, looking down at our children playing on the carpet. We have a three-year-old boy and a two-year-old girl, both of them beautiful children and look exactly like my husband. I kneel in front of my son, his small face coming toward me.

"Look, Mommy! I got a new car!" He shows me his toy, his face lighting up as he speaks about it.

I giggle as I take the toy from him. "Wow! Did your father get this for you?" I look over at my husband, who's beaming at us.

"We bought it from the toy store yesterday..." He stands up and starts to head toward the front door, fixing his tie on the way. "I'm heading to work now... Also, I found your old phone in the attic. I'm not sure if you want to look at it or not. It's on the kitchen counter."

Getting back onto my feet, I go to see my husband off, shutting the door tightly behind him. I think to myself for a moment... Do I really want to look at that phone? I know it will only bring back memories that I had worked so hard to bury.

However, I can't bring myself to ignore my feelings any longer. I rush into the kitchen, spotting the phone on the side of the counter.

As I pick it up, the memories of my past life all flood back to me. All of my friends... Him. I feel a shiver run down my spine as I remember the sound of his voice, and the feeling of his fingers against my skin. Mentally scolding myself for even thinking such things about another man, I click the on button. As I expected, it's dead. I search through the kitchen drawers, desperately trying to find a charger that will be able to fit the phone.

It doesn't take me long to find something, and I plug it in, my heart beating quickly. I don't know what I will find on here. I don't even know if everything will be as I left it. As I ponder, I see the icon that signals that the phone is turning on, and then the lock screen. The picture is of Felix, my best friend at the time, and the only one I had ever felt strongly toward.

As I stare at his face, my heart begins to drop. All this time, I've been trying to hide how much I miss him, and suddenly, all the agony of the situation hits me. My heart aches to hear the sound of his voice again, or even to see a text message from him.

WE MET BACK in middle school when he joined my class quite early into the year. He was a transfer student from Sweden and didn't know English very well. Since I was one of the more outgoing students, he was placed under my care, and we quickly became friends. I think that's when I started to fall in love with him but didn't realize it since I was so young.

I remember being incredibly fond of him, feelings that I didn't quite understand back then, but they're clear to me now.

We spent every break we had together, just talking about random things, making daisy chains on the field during the summer. I can vividly remember the way his eyes lit up when I placed one that I'd made onto his beautiful blonde hair.

I enjoyed middle school. We'd spent so much time together after school and during. I had lots of other friends apart from him, but he became my favorite quickly after we had first met. I tried to introduce him to my other friends, but they never really got along very well since he didn't understand them.

So, we spent most of our time alone. I tried my best to teach him my language as best I could. Surprisingly, he learned very quickly and could speak clearly to me in no time. The first time he ever made my heart, really beat, was when he pulled me into a big hug, letting me rest my head on his as we embraced. I was taller than him at the time, but he quickly grew to be much bigger than me. We stayed in that hug for a while. I still don't really know why he decided to do it. Maybe he just wasn't feeling well that day.

AFTER SEEING THAT PICTURE, I become curious. I want to see more of him. To reminisce on the old times that we had. Swallowing, I click on the photo icon. My eyes are suddenly flooded with pictures of us. Me and my best friend. The best friend whom I was in love with. Whom I'm still in love with.

One of the pictures stick out to me, and I press on it to get a closer look. It's a picture of us both sleeping, taken by another one of our friends at the time.

Back in high school, we had a sleepover at one of our friend's house with a few other people while her parents were out of town. We shared the couch downstairs, and I comfortably rested in his arms the whole night. That's when we shared our first kiss, too, during a classic game of spin the bottle.

Looking back on it now, I can see why our friends tried their hardest to get us together. Despite their efforts though, and my own love for him, he never felt the same way. We took so many pictures that I barely know where to look.

I then scroll back to when we were in high school, when we had taken the most pictures and spent the most time together. There is a group photo with us and all of our high school friends, sitting on the track field for our last day of school picture. Unsurprisingly, Felix and I were cuddled together in the corner of the picture, with some of our friends looking at us fondly.

Chapter Two

I didn't enjoy high school as much as I'd expected to. The days dragged, and I struggled to make a lot of friends. I only had a couple, whom I'd only really met because Felix had made friends with them first. They were a couple of girls, which we grew incredibly close with over time. But still, we were never as close as I was with Felix.

Felix always stayed by my side, defending me from anyone who tried to pick a fight with me. I didn't really have that many arguments with people. I was quieter and tended to keep to myself. But there was one girl who didn't like me at all. I don't personally remember doing anything to annoy her; she had just seemingly taken a disliking to me for no reason. She would pull my hair and shout insults at me.

Now, thinking back, maybe she was jealous; what other reason could there have been? But it made me feel terrible. At first, it didn't bother me that much; I was able to ignore it. But it soon became worse and worse when her friends sometimes joined in.

But she would never say anything to me when Felix was

around, so I'd purposely keep to his side as much as possible to avoid her.

One day though, he finally noticed what was going on when she shouted something at me without realizing that he was nearby. I will always remember how his face twisted into a glare when he realized what she had said. I'd never seen him that angry before. Well, I'd never seen him angry, period. He was always happy, so optimistic.

It resulted in him snapping at her, and she broke down in front of everyone. She was the typical high school bully, so a couple of people chuckled, causing her to get even more upset. The girl never said anything to me again after that, but she always looked like she was carrying a hateful word on her shoulder. Not that I cared much.

One of her friends actually came up to me after that, apologizing for how she had treated me. She told me how much she hated the way they treated people and asked if we could become friends. Of course, I said yes, eager to invite her into my circle. We became very close friends after that, and she actually attended my wedding.

Everything that I had gone through with my parents and other people had convinced me that I didn't deserve his affection, but he always assured me that it was sort of a "thank you" for helping him learn English, and being one of the only people who truly bothered to befriend him. Even though high school wasn't a very memorable experience for me, I do remember being extremely happy with my life. At least, in comparison to how my life actually turned out.

Sure, I love my husband very much, and now that we're married, I wouldn't want to change him for the world. But I still feel robbed of my chance with Felix, even after all this time away from him. I'm still curious about what he could possibly be doing with his life right now.

I continue to flick through the gallery. The way his eyes

look at me so lovingly in all of the photos makes me question his feelings, too... But maybe, I was just being hopeful; it's too late now, anyway. Another one of the photos show us eating ice cream together, with some cringey stickers and filters all over the screen.

We were in high school; who could blame us?

Back then, my parents weren't the best, and I had problems with them all the time. We had tons of arguments, which ultimately ended in me getting kicked out of their home constantly. Felix gave me a place to stay, meaning, we spent most of our time together. Ultimately, my feelings for him became stronger, and I became more and more attached to him.

Even though my home life was bad, Felix and his parents made it a lot better. I felt comfortable at his house and was allowed to stay whenever I needed to. My parents were going through a pretty rough divorce, and I seemingly "got in the way" — their words — so Felix gave me a place to stay while they recovered and regained their time for me.

The time we spent at his house wasn't very eventful. He still only saw me as his best friend, so the most we ever did was cuddle and watch endless amounts of movies. But it was enough to make me extremely happy at the time. I would lay my head on his chest and listen to the sound of his heart beating peacefully. His hand would wrap around my waist and pull me closer to him. We would also sleep like that, too, his arms around me and my arms around him.

Back then, I was convinced that he would be able to hear the sound of my heartbeat from where he lied. It was beating so loudly from the experience, and I could only hope that he didn't realize how nervous I was.

I CLUTCH onto the cabinets as I feel my knees weaken. My head feels so hot, and my heart is throbbing. Why is this happening? Part of me wishes that my husband had left the phone in the attic, along with everything I still feel for Felix. But another part of me is grateful.

To this day, I still miss him. In the end, I never even got a chance to say goodbye to him. It was so strange, the way we could go from being best friends to being strangers within minutes.

The sound of my son crying suddenly distracts me from my thoughts. I place the phone down on the counter so it can charge, and I go to check on him.

"Are you hungry?" I ask as I pick him up from the ground, taking him to the kitchen for breakfast.

I place him in his highchair and pour out a bowl of cereal and milk. As I go to give it to him, I notice something. His blonde hair looks just like Felix's, and the loving look in his eyes as he stare at me is also the same.

I must've been staring for a short while, because he starts to speak. "Mommy?"

"Sorry." I shake the thought from my head and place the bowl on the highchair, along with a plastic spoon for him to eat with.

Now, everything I look at reminds me of him. Even the countertops remind me of when we would bake cookies together, and he'd lift me up to sit on top of it like a child. He always said that it was to get me out of the way. Thinking back on it now, it makes me chuckle. I can finally see why our friends thought we had something.

My son finishes up with his meal, and I let him out of the chair, placing the bowl into the sink to be washed later. Now that the children are busy, I have another chance to look through the phone. Picking it up once again, I open my messages, desperate to look at what we used to talk about.

When the texts eventually load, I'm able to read the last few ones we ever sent to each other.

LAUREN

I hope I can see you again soon :)
Goodnight, please sleep well.

FELIX

We'll meet again soon! I'll only stay here for a short while so I can visit my grandparents, and then we'll finally be reunited.
Goodnight, love.

We never spoke again after that. I heard from another friend that he met some girl while he was back home visiting his grandparents, and decided that he was going to stay with her. He felt too guilty to speak to me himself, so he stuck to communicating through our friends, which I hated.

I scroll up a few months, before he went away, to one of my favorite memories. One that I will never be able to forget, no matter how much I try to force myself to. I find what I'm looking for and begin to read through the messages.

FELIX

I'm sorry about what happened… We were both really drunk, and I guess what happened, happened. Let's just forget about it, okay?

The first time we went out to drink as legal adults ended in us getting carried away and spending the night together. Secretly, I wanted us to pursue what happened further, and finally make things official, but I could've never said that to him. Before all of that happened, however, I did make an attempt to tell him my feelings, but it didn't go how I had expected, and he shrugged me off.

I find the chat, exhaling loudly as I remember the pain I felt back then.

LAUREN

> Do you really love me, Felix? I love you so much that it hurts, and I can't keep acting like I don't.

FELIX

> Of course, I do. You're my best friend, after all :) Did something happen?

LAUREN

> No, my day just hasn't been great. I'm going to sleep now.

FELIX

> Sleep well. I'll see you in the morning.

After that experience, it was clear to me that he didn't want anything more than what we already had. I felt so stupid that seeing him every day after that just felt embarrassing, and he still has no idea how I feel.

Or maybe he does, and just chooses to ignore it.

Chapter Three

We didn't have many classes together in college. I only saw him when our breaks lined up. And we tried our best to see each other as much as we could. However, he became pretty popular in college, with girls constantly trying to get with him. Of course, this made me extremely jealous, and I subtly tried to make it seem like he already had a girlfriend so they'd leave him alone.

I'd give him my hair ties and bracelets to wear on his wrists. Rings for his fingers. "Accidentally" spray him with my perfume. But nothing really fully kept everyone away from him, and he didn't wear them often. I wonder if he still has them?

There was this one girl who was totally infatuated with him, and she constantly messaged him and tried to hang out with us. Every time I saw her, I acted extra clingy around him, holding onto his arms, hugging him. It got to the point where she asked me herself if we were dating, since she wanted to ask him out. I absent-mindedly told her that we were so she wouldn't make an attempt at getting together with him.

The next day, he asked me why I told her that we were

dating. That's when I broke down. I remember crying more than I ever had before, and telling him that I was terrified of being replaced with someone else. He told me he didn't like her anyway, and she left us alone.

Along with everything else that happened in college, we stayed great friends. I managed to make a few new friends of my own, but Felix never really spoke that often with them since I wanted to keep him all for myself. It sounds selfish now, but at the time, I was so in love with him that I didn't care. I don't think I remember arguing with him once the whole time we were friends. After everything we had been through, I was convinced that he was my soulmate. And that if I was patient enough, everything would fall into place, and we could spend our lives together.

At least, I was hopeful back then. I don't think I would've made it through the long days without crying, otherwise. The way my heart yearned for him to become mine made me feel awful. But the things he did would make me happier than ever. So, I couldn't get enough of him and his presence.

Once college was over, we each got different jobs and agreed that when we earned enough money, we would buy a house and move in together. I remember him explaining to me how he wanted his wedding to be, what he wanted his kids to be like. As much as I wanted to ask him to share his life with me, I didn't, and instead, spoke about my own ideas for a wedding, which were pretty similar to his. I saved up a lot of money for our house, and that was when he told me he was going back to Sweden to see his family. The news that broke my heart.

But we made a promise to see each other again soon, and then we would be able to move in together and start building a life together as best friends.

But that day never came. The stories I heard about him were all different. I never did see him again. However, if the story about him meeting another girl back home was true, I hope she treats him well. I hope she loves him as much as I have loved him during all these years.

After I heard that news, I cried for weeks. My mind couldn't think about anyone else but the man whom I've pursued my whole life, falling in love with someone else. I went into the dating game, trying everything I could to forget about him, burying away the memories that we created together. I threw my phone away and started anew, vowing to never think about or contact him again. As much as it killed me, I needed to do it for my own happiness.

I met Clarke, my husband, during that time, too. I loved him, obviously. But as guilty as I am to say this, I don't think I love him as much as I'd loved, and still love, Felix. I don't think I could ever love anyone as much as I love him. I don't want to say that I regret my marriage to my husband, but the feeling dawns on me.

Despite this, I have no way of ever contacting Felix again, so moving on is my only hope at living a normal life.

I TURN the phone off and place it to one side of the counter, feeling dizzy from the overwhelming number of emotions currently residing in my body. I crave seeing other things that I can remember him by, anything other than this phone. Things that are much more personal.

Gulping, I make my way toward the attic. I had kept some things up there when he left, even though I tried to convince myself to get rid of them so I could forget. I couldn't bring myself to do it and kept everything instead in a big box, which I hid in the attic.

I pull down the ladder and start to climb up, watching my step on the way up. I'm not as agile as I used to be.

Once I'm up, I turn on the lightbulb and look around, silently praying that Clarke hadn't meddled in my old boxes and thrown them away. Fortunately, my eyes land upon a carboard box, which has the word "memories" sprawled across the side of it in black sharpie ink. That's exactly what I'm looking for.

Moving some of the other things out of the way, I pull the box toward me, sitting down beside it and pulling open the lid, immediately greeted with an old, familiar scent.

The first thing I lay my hand on is an old diary. I remember that I had written about him a lot in here during high school. I open the first page, listening to the crackle of the spine as I do so. Seeing my old handwriting on the page really takes me back. It's surprising how much handwriting can change over time.

I take a moment to read through the diary, remembering all of the events that happened in there as clear as day.

December 11, 2001

Today was boring. I saw Felix a lot, though! Our class was cancelled, so we ended up sitting outside the classroom and sharing a snack while we waited for the day to end. It was a new type of food from his home country. I can't remember the name, though; it was something complicated.

December 12, 2001

It's finally Friday! Felix invited me to stay over at his house during the weekend since my parents are arguing again (no surprise there).

But I'm happy that we can spend time together; he makes me so happy. I'm glad we're friends. Tonight, we're going to bake cookies and watch lots of movies.

December 14, 2001

I couldn't write over the weekend since I wasn't at home, but I had a great time at Felix's! We watched so many movies, and his parents are great cooks. I ate so much good food that I felt like my stomach was going to explode.

I took a shower at his house and used some of his shampoo, so my hair smells just like him now. I don't think I'll be washing it for a while. I'm wearing his clothes, too. They're kind of baggy on me. It's weird that I used to be so much bigger than him at the start of high school.

Last night, his parents asked us if we think we'll be friends forever. And Felix said yes! That made me smile. Although, I hope that we can become something more than just friends soon... Maybe we can date?

December 15, 2001

I hate Mondays. We have this really awful teacher who hates me for no reason at all. Every

time I try to speak to him, he ignores me. He
adores Felix, though. I wonder what it's like to
be liked by absolutely everyone… Felix and I
made a daisy chain during lunch, though, so
that was nice. We got carried away, and it
ended up being really long!

I skip through a few pages in the diary, trying to find
something interesting inside. I then come across a particular
page that's covered in smudged ink and wet stains, hinting that
I had indeed been crying on this page.

January 10, 2002
I love Felix so much. But he will never know
that because I'm too scared to tell him. I'm
terrified of losing him, and it seems like no
matter what I do, he will drift away from me.
I wish I knew how to keep him to myself
forever. Every time I think about him, my heart
aches. I feel so stupid; how could I have
fallen this deeply in love with my best friend?
I haven't slept properly in days because I'm
terrified of him replacing me with somebody
else.

January 11, 2002
I feel much better today. I spoke to Felix
about my feelings a little… He assured me that

he won't ever replace me with anyone else, and I'll always be his bestest friend. Still, I haven't confessed my feelings to him yet. I don't think I ever will, only in my dreams. I had a good dream last night. I got married to Felix, we had two children, and were happy and in love. I'd like to think that's our future, and I'm some sort of fortune teller. We are soulmates, after all.

January 12, 2002

Today was so scary. Felix almost read my diary! I invited him over to my house for a while, which is rare because my parents never let us see each other. But they're out of town right now. Anyway, I asked him to grab something for me out of my bedside drawer. That is the drawer in which I keep this diary! I'm so dumb; I should have thought about that before asking him. He picked it up and asked, "What's this?" And opened the first page! I had to grab it away from him quickly and say that I wrote about some private stuff in there that he wouldn't want to know about. That could've been so embarrassing...

January 13, 2002

Felix ended up staying the night since it started to rain, and I didn't want him to walk home in the rain. I had to sneak him out in the morning, though. If my parents ever find out I had a boy in the house overnight, I'm certain that they'll kill me.

Oh, well, at least last night was fun. We talked about some fun stuff, about what type of wedding we want! And baby names. I'm not sure if I'd want any children in the future; they seem like a pain. But if they were with Felix, it would be okay, I think. Everyone loves Felix! I don't know whether I'm happy about that or not...

Closing the diary, I rummage through the box, certain that I had kept the daisy chain that we made during that one lunch. The memories are all flowing back to me now. I can remember everything that we did together, and it makes me sad. But reminiscing on the past is good sometimes, I think. It helps you to appreciate it more. I finally find the daisy chain and pull it out of the box.

The daisy chain is completely squashed from being in that box for such a long time. Plus, the flowers are dead (which is no surprise), but I can still remember when we made it. He would pass me the daisies he had picked from the grass bank. Our fingers would touch for a moment while I took it from him, and I would add it to our chain. We ended up doing that during most of our break, so it got pretty long.

I gently place the daisy chain down on the ground. I definitely should have found a way to preserve it better. But it doesn't matter now. I dig my hand into the box and pull out a piece of paper. It's thick and crumpled, with some of the ink smudged down the page. Looking at the drawing, I can tell that it was a drawing of me. Short, straight blonde hair, brown eyes. It's a picture that Felix had drawn of me while I was sleeping at his house.

He had always enjoyed art, and sketched a lot even in middle school. In this picture, I was wrapped up in his blankets, my mouth slightly agape as I did so. At the time, I almost cried when he showed it to me and told me to keep it. But I kept my cool.

Chuckling at the memory, I place it down and reach my hand into the box to try and find something else.

My hand lands on a small jewelry box, and I can immediately tell what it is. I flick open the velvet lid to reveal a silver necklace. My birthday present. When Felix had given it to me, he told me to close my eyes and hold up my hair, to which I did. And then he wrapped it around my neck, clipping it gently around me. There was a locket attached to it, which contained a picture of us both. The gift meant the world to me, and I wore it everywhere. Only stopping when I heard about him meeting somebody new.

As much as I love Felix, he confuses me. I thought that we were something more than just friends, always. The way he treated me signaled that we were something more. The hugs he gave me weren't just friendly. Our first times for everything were with each other. I rejected every boy who tried to make a move on me, all because I thought I would have a chance with him.

Chapter Four

To this day, I still blame myself for that. I still think that my confession could've been better, or I should have messaged him more when he was away to prevent us from drifting apart like we did. I couldn't even do anything to stop us from drifting, but instead, I just sat and cried.

Letting out a sigh, I place the jewelry box on the ground beside the diary and daisy chain. Something else in the box catches my eye. It's a little pink dinosaur plushie. Like the ones that you win at the fair. Felix had one, too, but his was blue. We both decided to name them after each other, and promised to keep them forever. I do still wonder if he kept that promise. I'm sure he did.

I hold the plushie in my hand, squeezing it a little, and it still feels soft. Even though it had been in my attic all this time. As for how we got them, we actually won them at a fair. Well, Felix did. It was a game of basketball. Dunk one, and get a prize. Of course, Felix won. He was seemingly good at every-thing, after all. He won one for me, and one for himself. That was also when we promised to keep them forever.

During our time at the fair, we tried to ride everything. Just to get our money's worth. It was fun, though. I spent my time clinging onto Felix's hands on the bigger rides. Not because I was scared, but because I wanted some kind of excuse to hold him. His hands felt so warm in the freezing cold weather.

I pull out something else, something that, even now, makes me blush. It's a pregnancy test, and it's positive. But it had turned out to be wrong once we got to the hospital.

When Felix and I spent that night together, we didn't bother to use any kind of protection since we were both too drunk to even comprehend the situation. But I can still remember the passionate way he kissed me. I should've known then that he loved me like I loved him. No one kisses their best friend that way.

Now, it seems strange to save something like this, but I never want to forget that time we spent together. I thought that I would've been relieved when the doctors told me that I was certainly not pregnant. But instead, I felt a little disappointed. I wouldn't have been opposed to having a child with him. But even if I were truly pregnant, I wouldn't have known what to do.

It was hard when I had my first child with Clarke. It would've been unimaginable if I'd had a child when I was that young. I remember Felix being terrified, more scared than I was. Maybe because he didn't want a child when we were still in college. It was understandable, after all.

Everything that had happened between us back then didn't matter anymore. Our childhood was over, just like the tight bond that we had shared. I knew that nothing was bound to last forever, but I was convinced that we would be the ones who did.

I start to place everything I had pulled out back into the

box, taking one last look at the memories I was putting away. This time, hopefully, forever.

I hear the front door open and rush back down the stairs, returning the ladder to its natural state. I can't have Clarke knowing about my feelings for my best friend. I feel a tear run down my right cheek as I hear him greet our children. I feel so guilty for regretting my marriage with him...

If I had confessed to Felix properly, would things be different now? Quickly, I wipe away my tears and try to ignore the aching feeling inside my heart. Time had flown by while I was thinking about my old life with Felix, and before I knew it, it's time to face my husband. The marriage that I am now finding myself regretting after all these years.

In fact, despite my feelings now, I did have the picture-perfect wedding that I had described to Felix, just without him. I had the perfect children that I had once described to Felix, just not with him like I had always hoped. I'm aware that I'd made some mistakes along the way during my lifetime. I only wish that I had at least stayed in contact with him, even if we just stayed friends. I crave his presence again, and I want to know if he's doing okay.

"Honey, did you have a good day?" Clarke smiles at me when our eyes meet, his hands placing themselves on my waist.

"Yeah, it was okay."

His eyes then land on the phone behind me. "Did you look through the phone?"

I nod. "I looked through it. There's nothing important on there. You can get rid of it, only old high school memories that I'd like to forget."

All the pictures with him, the messages, everything, will die, along with this phone.

"Alright, then. I'll get rid of it." He picks the phone up off the kitchen counter and click the on button. "I'll have to restore it to its factory settings first. Meaning that everything on here will be unrecoverable... Is there anything you'd like to take off here first?"

I shake my head. "It's all just old junk that I don't need anymore."

"What's the password?"

I take the phone from his hand and type in the password, looking at the picture of me and Felix one more time before giving it back to him.

"Thank you..." He looks at the phone for a moment. "I was thinking. You've never mentioned a guy like this before. Was he your old boyfriend or something?"

I let out a sad chuckle. "No, he was just my friend..."

I try to hold back more tears... My boyfriend? My soulmate? My best friend? I have no idea. I'm still confused, even after all this time... Pathetic.

"Then I'll go ahead and delete everything, and we can go sell it in the morning. We might even be able to get some money back."

He gives me a smile, and I watch as he clicks the factory reset button. My heart is pounding in my chest. Am I making the right decision here?

My husband places the phone in his pocket and goes to check on the children, leaving me in the kitchen with my thoughts.

I'd like to think that my friendship with Felix never ended. We never argued, simply just drifted. And if we ever meet again, which is very unlikely... we will become good friends again.

It's too late to pursue a relationship now. But I'll be happy just to see his face again.

There's one last thing I need to do before my past can be fully erased... I follow my husband into the living room to see him holding our son.

"Honey... I checked the attic earlier, and there are some

boxes that I need to get rid of. Will you help me carry them to the car?"

All that's left is to erase my high school self. The diary, the daisy chain, the drawing, the necklace, the plushie. I will never truly be free unless they are all gone, too. I feel my heart break a little when I see my husband turn his head and give me a small nod.

"Show me what I'm bringing down, and we'll take it right away. The kids can come, too. It will be good for them to get some fresh air."

We both head up to the attic. The whole way there, I question my decision, but it's something I know I need to do. To kill off the memories that have been stopping me from living my life this whole time. I point to the box that I had been looking at earlier. The box full of my memories.

My husband crouches down beside the box, reading the text written along the side of it. "Memories? Are you sure that you want to get rid of this?"

He tries to open the box to look inside, but I stop him. I can't show him my past. I won't! What will he think of me if he finds out that I'm still hung up on my childhood best friend?

My hand grips onto his, stopping him from looking inside. "Yeah. There's nothing really in there. Nothing that I need. It's just junk. You've saved a lot of trash from when you were young. I'm sure you know what I mean." I give him a small, fake smile.

Choosing not to question me anymore, he picks up the box and places it under his arm. "Anything else?"

"No. That's it. Will you give me a moment? I need to check some things, and then I'll meet you at the car."

He nods and carefully heads down. I hear him call the kids' names for a brief moment before it goes completely silent. I collapse onto the attic floor, my eyes filling up with tears. My body aches, and my head feels like it could explode any minute. Why does it have to end like this? I was so happy with him.

"Why did you leave me?!" I scream out, my hands clutching tightly at my shirt.

I let the tears flow down my face, the tears that I had worked so hard to keep in all this time. I even wanted to cry on my own wedding day, and when my children were born. All because I felt like I was with the wrong person. I'm still so attached to Felix, even though he's thousands of miles away now, impossible to find.

I take a minute to clean myself up. I need to face the present now and stop dwelling on the past. Felix is gone, along with all of our memories. After everything we had gone through, I hope Felix is living a happy, fulfilling life. And I hope that he still thinks about me and the life we shared from time to time. But no matter how much I want to forget about him and move on with my own life, just like he has, I can't help but feel desperate to tell him the words "I love you" one more time.

And this time, it will be for real...

I rub my eyes and climb down the ladder. There is just one thing that I want to take out of the box. Now that my decision on what I will do next is final, I want to take one thing with me. I open the trunk of the car and search through the box until I find the jewelry box. Taking out the necklace, I look at the picture in the locket one last time.

Felix knew that this picture is my favorite of us. It shows the both of us in his parents' car, heading to the beach. We were both smiling and eating ice cream. That was one of those times when I was truly happy. I close the locket and clasp it around my neck, not having Felix to help me do it this time. I adjust it, and then go to sit in the passenger seat of the car, beside my husband.

"Are you ready? You sure you want to throw that stuff out?" His eyes wander to the necklace that I am now wearing, and I quickly cover it with my hand.

"I'm ready... Let's go." I want to get this over with as quickly as possible.

My heart already aches, and I can't wait for it to stop for good.

The drive to the dumping site is becoming one of the longest drives of my life. The car is almost completely silent, the quiet sound of the radio the only thing keeping me from going completely insane. My heart is beating out of my chest, and I can feel it against my fingers as I hold onto the locket.

I stare out the window the whole time, passing by all of the happy families. I feel terrible. I had ruined our perfect relationship with my stupid feelings. Otherwise, we would be just like those happy couples.

Finally, we arrive at the site. Clarke tries to get out of the car, but I stop him.

"Let me take it; I'll be alright."

Without waiting for him to respond, I climb out of the car, slamming the door behind me, and headed toward the trunk. Opening it up, my eyes glance at the box. "Memories" was still written on the side. I grab the box and carry it toward one of the garbage bins, my hands clutching tightly against the cardboard. Now that I'm actually doing it, it feels wrong. But this is the only way.

Without dwelling on it any further, I heave the box toward the bin, watching as it gets lost in the heaps and mounds of cardboard. You can barely even tell them apart now, my whole childhood mixed with a bunch of old, dirty cardboard boxes. Not turning back, I head back to the car, my husband looking at me worriedly the whole way.

Once I sit back down, my husband places his hand on my knee gently. "Are you okay? You look upset, and your eyes are all puffy and red..." He pauses for a moment to look outside at the dumping site. "What did you throw away?"

"I told you; it's just a box." I turn to face him, and our eyes meet for a moment.

I quickly turn away from him again. The pain is too unbearable. I can't even love my own husband anymore, not after everything I had remembered today.

"Do you want to talk about it?" His hand leaves my knee and caresses the locket on my necklace.

I shake my head and quickly pull away from him. "I'm going to walk home. I need some time alone. Besides, it's not a long walk." I push open the car door, hesitating for a second before turning back to give my husband a kiss on the cheek.

"Do you want to take the kids with you? For company?"

"Take them home. I have some things I need to take care of before I head back."

I stretch over to the back seat to cover my children in kisses before I leave. It will be my last chance, after all.

I climb out of the car and wave goodbye to them, a single tear falling down my face. As I clutch onto the locket and walk, I think about how selfish I'm being. Choosing to leave a caring husband and beautiful children behind, all for someone I no longer even associate with. But the pain is so bad; I want it all to be over.

Walking in the opposite direction of my home, I stare upwards at the clouds, trying to make shapes out of them. Just like I used to do with Felix. In fact, I can almost hear him say, "Look! A sheep!"

Today, I will make sure that those memories die alongside me. I can't face anything anymore. I have become way too reliant on someone who is completely out of my reach. Someone who has moved on from me and our life together.

When today is over, I hope that I can be reborn. And I can finally live the life I had hoped for with Felix. Maybe this time around, it will be perfect. The perfect wedding, beautiful children we pick out baby names together for.

And if I'm not reborn with Felix, I'll do this over and over, an endless cycle to ensure our happiness. If I get the opportunity to do all of this again, to relive my time with Felix, I will do it right. I will do everything in my power to make him stay.

I will stay by his side forever.

The End

In Love with my Best Friend

Three Little Words

TROUBLED GIRLS FIND LOVE

Three Little Words

Three Little Words Blurb

I always thought Parker was the one, the other half of my heart, the one I dreamt night after night about raising a family with.

Until I found out that he'd been f*cking Stephanie... among others.

Fifteen years.

After fifteen soul-sucking years of being with the same guy, I now find myself **back in the dating world**.

First, it's Matthew, a data engineer whom I instantly connected with.

Until I stupidly said those three words, those **dreaded three words** that had him bolting out the restaurant doors.
I love you.

Guy after guy I'd meet, all heading for the hills.
Until Rodney Hersey comes along. Charming, sexy, and **he loves me back!**

Who would've thought?!

Immediately, I find myself dangling from his lips, tearing off my clothes, even getting married... after only one date!
But my life turns dark when I wake up in a strange home surrounded by four other women... *all claiming to be Rodney's wife.*

What have I gotten myself into?

A dark, short story about what happens when you say "I love you" to the wrong person.

Chapter One

Fifteen Years. Parker had taken fifteen years from her. Fifteen years that she'd never get back. It all started when they were fifteen and entirely too young and too immature to see anything else past their lustful love for each other. They had been friends ever since the seventh grade.

Veronica had been seated beside Parker in their math class. She was always good at math, her mind proving to be nothing if not analytical. Parker, on the other hand, he preferred sports, history, and government.

"Hey, I'm Parker," he introduced himself. He was so lean and scrawny then. His voice was even higher pitched, as all the other middle school boys fell victim to, also.

Veronica tucked her hair behind her ear. "I'm Veronica," she murmured.

Parker leaned in close, closer than he should have with a stranger. He didn't seem to notice, but she did. She could practically taste the cologne emanating from his shirt.

"I have to let you know," he whispered, "I'm not very good at math. Never have been. So, I might have to lean on you a little."

Veronica could barely breathe. She thought back to that very moment years later and wondered if he was just using her from the beginning. Most likely, he was telling her this because he wanted to copy her answers. He wanted to give her a heads up that he wouldn't try to hide his need for "help." He probably wasn't trying to make a move on her or even flirt. But twelve-year-old Veronica ignored that. She was just happy to be spoken to. Especially by someone so popular, so charming, and so... good looking.

She let out a breathy chuckle. "That's okay. I can help you."

That grin — that wide, crooked grin as bright as the sun — with dimples lining each side in his rounded cheeks... she didn't stand a chance.

They bonded over math homework, juicy gossip amongst their friends, and after school sports. Veronica helped Parker with his math assignments, and if he fell short, she let him copy her answers. In turn, Parker invited her to his soccer games and convinced her to join him and his friends during their breaks. She helped him, and he helped her right back.

At first, it just seemed like a transfer of services. Parker needed help in class, and she could offer help. She was awkward and lonely without any real friends of her own, so he brought her into his circle. But as they spent more and more time together, she started to grow fond of him.

Parker was easy to talk to, something Veronica needed with her social anxiety and unconventional conversational skills. He was warm and bubbly and eager to draw her in closer. Even if his friends, especially the girls, weren't always the warmest toward her, Parker was always sweet. He smiled whenever they made eye contact in the halls. He laughed at all her bad jokes. He didn't tease her too much when she utterly failed at playing soccer with him one time after school. And her name on his lips...

"Veronica... I like you. Will you go out with me?" he asked her during their sophomore year of high school.

FRESHMAN YEAR WAS rough as they both adjusted to new schools, new teachers, friends leaving and new friends being made, and their interests dividing them more. Parker joined the varsity soccer team, something unheard of among most freshmen, and he was praised as a soccer god. He walked the halls proud, confident, and that grin of his drawing girls to him like the plague.

But it wasn't just his grin, his whole body changed when puberty hit. He grew nearly a foot, his voice deepened to a husky baritone. He grew out his hair so it hung in shaggy brown curls around his sharp jaw line and tanned face. After joining the soccer team, he started working out at the gym more, and he packed on lean muscle to accentuate his new physique.

He was the talk of the school, and Veronica fell behind, clouded over in the shadows. She joined the math team and the chess team, and quickly became a leader in their competitions. To help herself become more comfortable in social situations, she joined the debate team, too. That really forced her out of her shell and allowed her to make new, accepting friends. She was happy with this new life, and she was on a clear path forward, but something was missing. She figured that out whenever she saw Parker's bright grin down a packed hallway. He was never far away, but never close enough to reach.

By the beginning of sophomore year, she abandoned all hope that Parker would return to her life. But fate played games and had other plans for her.

One day during gym class, they were told that they would

be playing soccer. Veronica groaned, but everyone else started easily enough. Parker, as one might imagine, was thrilled, and he dominated the field. She tried to avoid him as best she could, but as her team climbed the ranks, and Parker's team had an obvious winning streak, the two met head-to-head in the final bracket.

Seeing as how she was useful in no other position on the field, her team deemed her their goalie. They did a fairly good job of keeping the ball away from her, and she was grateful. But against Parker, they didn't stand a chance. She tried to block his shots, and when that failed, she tried to confront him on the field before he reached the goal. But he easily went around her. He had no mercy, no compassion. Her blood heated, and she was determined to stop one thing that day. Even if it was only one ball, she would stop him in his tracks. She would show him and everyone else watching, that he was not unstoppable.

And so, she did.

Parker came sprinting down the field, soccer ball kept close to his feet. He dodged a defender, and then faked past another. He came closer and closer to the goal, and Veronica tensed. Parker's foot raised, and then the ball came flying at her like a bullet. She jumped in its direction, and she stopped it. Everyone went quiet around her; the light from the shining afternoon sun even dimmed.

She heard her name being called from somewhere in the distance, but her vision swirled and darkened at the corners as she tried to find the source of the deep voice. She could remember nothing from that moment to when she woke up later in the nurse's office, a thick bandage on her head and a chip in her tooth. Parker sat beside her bed on a plastic chair. He wrung his hands together again and again as his foot tapped on the floor.

She cleared her throat.

"Veronica! You're awake!" He jumped up, grabbing her hand. "Oh, God. Thank God! I was worried you'd never wake up after... well..."

Veronica touched her head as her last memory of the soccer ball flying full speed at her face flashed in her mind. She flinched at her soft finger's touch.

"What happened?" she whispered.

Parker rubbed at his neck. "I, um, I got a little carried away during gym class. The ball — it hit you on the head and knocked you out. The nurse... she thinks you might have a concussion. I shouldn't have shot that ball so hard. I hit you, and I hurt you, and... I'm so sorry, Veronica. I didn't mean—"

"Parker." She squeezed his hand gently. He peered down at her light touch. "It's okay. I'm alright. It was an accident."

Parker wavered, but she gave him her best smile, ignoring the pounding pain in her head.

"Okay," he whispered.

"Hey," she said, "remember when you tried to teach me how to play soccer in the seventh grade?"

He chuckled lightly. "Yeah. You weren't terrible."

"I was awful!" She laughed. "I tripped over the ball and fell face first into the mud. I could taste mud in my mouth for the next two days."

Parker's face split into a wide grin. His chest rolled with deep belly laughs. "Your face when you looked up at me — it was covered in mud. And that little glop dripped from your nose—" His laugh exploded out of him. "Oh, God. I couldn't hold it together. I felt so bad."

She smiled at him. Even if she had terribly embarrassed herself again in front of him, she was thankful to see his smile back.

After that, the two of them stayed camped out in the nurse's office until Veronica's mom came to pick her up two hours later. They chatted about school work, the classes they liked and didn't like, the people they called "friends," their extracurriculars, life at home... two hours stretched into an eternity, and yet was cut short. She could've stayed in that bed forever and talked to him. She missed his smile, his voice, his warm laugh, his teasing and jokes.

She missed him.

"Hey," she mumbled as her mom spoke to the nurse in the next room. "I, um, well, would you, um, maybe, you see, I—"

"Veronica," he cut her rambling short with a gentle smile. "I've missed you."

She swallowed past the lump in her throat. "I miss you, too," she whispered.

Parker smiled at her. "Can we hang out again soon? Can I text you?"

She nodded quickly, maybe a little too quickly. "Anytime, you know that."

She left that day with her mom and waved at Parker, thanking him for keeping her company. But that wasn't the last of them like she had half-expected.

Parker texted her that evening after school. And then the following morning. And then again during class. And then every moment of every day after.

They rejoiced like she had longed for, and then a week before homecoming, he met with her at the ice cream shop they frequented together. He bought a cone for her and licked at his own sundae. They ate in silence, and just when she was starting to think something was wrong, he took her hand in his, ice cream sundae forgotten completely.

"*Veronica*... I like you. Will you go out with me?" he asked her, his face abnormally serious.

She forced herself to swallow, but the ice cream burned with cold down her throat. She coughed and sputtered, and he handed her napkins.

"That bad?" He chuckled, but she could see the hurt

wavering in his eyes. She had never seen him so focused, so serious.

She waved her hands. "No, no! It was the ice cream. Parker, I... I like you, too," she mumbled.

Parker's smile blossomed. "You do?"

"I do." She blushed.

"So... will you go out with me? And, um... maybe be my date to homecoming?"

She nodded, not trusting her voice.

"Really? Really, really?"

She grinned then, the widest she ever had before. "Yes, Parker."

Parker scooped her into his arms and gave her the biggest bear hug. They finished their ice cream that night and talked in his car for hours afterward. They went to homecoming a week later. And then started junior year, and then senior. They went on countless dates. They hung out every chance they could. They hugged, kissed, and touched constantly. They were inseparable.

So, when they both graduated and found out that they were going to the same college, he asked her to move in with him, and she eagerly agreed. They finished college hand in hand and moved into their own apartment together after. Parker got a job in sports marketing, and Veronica became a data analyst. They bought new cars, they got a cat together, they filled their apartment with plants, with decorations, with love. And Veronica hoped that soon, they'd add children into the mix. It seemed inevitable. Almost as inevitable as the engagement ring on her finger now.

THEY HAD BEEN TOGETHER for fifteen years and had been engaged for one of those blissful years. Their marriage was planned for the spring. She had almost finished the arrangements and was finally starting to feel like she could relax and breathe again. But just as everything settled, she found purple lace panties in his sock drawer when she was putting away their laundry. She dropped them on the carpet.

Purple lace panties — that were *not* hers.

She sat on the edge of the bed all afternoon, silently staring at them on the floor. The sun shined high in the sky and flickered out into dusky shadows through the balcony door in their bedroom. And then, the front door clicked, and Parker stepped inside. He found her there, in the same position. But he didn't need to ask what was wrong when he found where her gaze landed.

"Whose are those?" she whispered, her voice croaking and thick with held back tears.

Parker audibly swallowed. "Veronica..."

"*Whose*, Parker?" She cut him off.

He sighed as he slipped his work bag over his head. He sat down beside her on the mattress and took her hand in his.

"They're Stephanie's, my... well, a woman I'm seeing."

Tears welled in Veronica's eyes. "Is she... the only one?"

At Parker's silence, she peered up at him. He flinched at her gaze. "No."

"How long?"

"Nine months," he conceded.

He had been cheating on her with multiple women... for nine months. While they were engaged. While she made wedding preparations. While she planned on bringing up the conversation of children... he was sleeping with other women.

She pushed herself up, wobbling only a little, and made her way to the door. Parker grabbed her hand.

"Veronica, wait! Can we... I mean... is this it, then? Aren't we going to talk about this?"

Veronica turned. She gave him the coldest, most distant stare she could muster. She wanted nothing more of him.

"You've made it pretty clear that this is it, don't you think?"

"Veronica, please. Let's talk about this."

She yanked her hand away from him. Parker's eyes widened, but she didn't care about the hurt she saw there. She just... didn't care anymore. She moved toward the door and heard Parker shuffling behind her, but he didn't go to grab her this time.

"Veronica! Please, just wait! Can't you just stop for a moment? Let me explain!"

Veronica propped the door open, her hand squeezing so tightly around the handle that her knuckles turned white as glue.

"I'm sorry I couldn't be enough for you," she let out. "But maybe Stephanie will be."

She clicked the door shut behind her and stepped down the hall. She left the shattered pieces of her past behind the door that day.

She didn't open it again.

Chapter Two

After being heartbroken by Parker, Veronica found it even more difficult than ever to meet and socialize with new, young suitors. Sure, she had bad social anxiety before, but after Parker's betrayal, she didn't know how to act around men. Was her flirting actually annoying them? Was her teasing too harsh? Was her quiet watchfulness not mysterious and humbling, but rather odd and awkward?

She had only one man in her life, one man to call her own — ever. Parker was her first everything — first kiss, first love, first roommate, and the one and only man she had ever slept with. He knew everything about her, and she him — or so she thought. She was comfortable with him. She came out of her hard shell for him, and she hadn't been back in since. But now that he was gone and out of the picture, she was left alone and confused.

She tried to talk to men at bars, and her friends from college pulled her along to clubs on the weekends. But as much as she boosted herself up and tried to fake confidence, she fell flat. The men she spoke to were nice at first, but the more she talked about her interests, her life, her past, and *Parker*... they put distance between themselves and her.

She reached out, trying to portray that fun-loving, friendly, carefree girl she had always been alongside Parker in high school, college, and then adulthood. But without him there, her crutch was removed, and she stumbled.

"Maybe you should try older men," her best friend, Maggie, suggested one evening at the club after Veronica had yet again struck out with a man.

She fumbled with her engagement ring in the front pocket of her bag. "I don't know. Maybe I'm just not cut out for dating."

"Nonsense!" Her other friend, Julia, yelled. "You'll find the right guy; it's just gonna take some time, girly. Don't let Parker and his wandering cock discourage you."

"But I just don't feel like myself. I can't talk to men, I've never been able to. Parker was a happy mistake, and he was the one who got me to come out of my shell in the first place."

Julia huffed, more than a little drunk. "*Parker* did nothing but tear your confidence down and make you question yourself."

"Yeah," Maggie chimed, sipping from her own drink. "You're better than that. You don't give yourself enough credit."

Veronica shrugged. "I don't know. Nothing I try is working."

"So, try online dating," Maggie said flatly. Both the other women looked at her. "What? Then you won't have to talk face-to-face with anyone unless you want to, and by then, you should have a better idea of what they're like and what they're into. Win-win."

Julia shrugged. "Not a bad idea, honestly."

Both her friends looked at her, and Veronica stared back as the gears in her head turned. She wouldn't have to go to clubs and bars and talk to total strangers. She wouldn't have to initiate conversation if she didn't want to. She didn't have to meet anyone she wasn't interested in. *And* she could talk to them anonymously until she was comfortable meeting up. Why hadn't she thought of doing this before?

"Let's do it." She smiled.

The three women downed their drinks after a short victory cheer. They left the club tipsy and stumbling over one another, but they quickly sobered up as they crashed on Maggie's couch in her apartment that evening. Julie got them all water bottles and snacks, and Maggie pulled up dating site after dating site. They worked together to make attractive, wholesome, and intriguing pages for Veronica, not without many snorting laughs and bubbling giggles.

By the end of the night, they had created three dating profiles for her on three different apps.

VERONICA FELL asleep on Maggie's couch that night and woke up the next morning to six messages from different men, all interested in her bio and wanted to get to know her better.

Veronica's lips curled into a smile as she scrolled through the compliments on her phone.

Her first in-person date with an online contact was with a man named Matthew. He was thirty-two, lived in the same city, worked as a data engineer for a large-scale company, and was into cheesy movies, hacking competitions, gaming, and robot fighting. He was smart, analytic, cute but in a nerdy kind of way, and very polite with every message he had sent via the dating app they used.

She was supposed to meet Matthew at a restaurant only a few blocks from her apartment. It was a small, local Mexican place that she suggested when he asked her to meet initially.

He agreed to meet her there at seven, so here she sat alone at a table, sipping on her glass of unsweet tea as the clock ticked closer and closer to seven. At five of, the door opened behind her. She glanced over her shoulder and, sure enough, the man from the pictures stepped inside. He ran a hand through his short blonde hair, and his blue eyes flickered around the main room from behind his round glasses.

She smiled and waved when she caught his gaze. He smiled right back as he sat down opposite her.

"Veronica?"

"That's me," she said lightly.

"It's a pleasure to finally meet you. You're even prettier than in your pictures." He flushed.

Her cheeks heated, too. "Thank you. You, um, aren't so bad yourself."

She eyed his tightly buttoned collared shirt that hung loosely around his lean chest. The golden watch around his thin, pale wrist. The blonde stubble that graced his jaw and neck. He looked like the opposite of Parker, but she still found herself attracted to him.

"So, you've been here before. What do you recommend for food?" He picked up the menu on the tabletop.

She pointed out two or three items that were worthwhile and recommended the house margarita if he wanted to enjoy a drink. He did, and he ordered exactly what she had told him to. She smiled at that.

"So, you're a data engineer. What exactly do you do?" she asked.

Matthew went into a long, drawn-out explanation of his job, to which any other person might have found boring, but seeing as her own position involved analyzing data, she was actually, honestly, interested. When he finished his rant, he asked her about her job, and she gladly told him about her work.

"It doesn't sound too different from mine." He chuckled.

She nodded, taking another sip of her water. "People always assume my job's boring and monotonous, but really, it's so interesting. I get to look for patterns in data, and from those patterns, draw conclusions that help consumers shop, and my company to better cater to their needs. I... well, I enjoy my job."

"I can tell. And I'm sure you're wonderful at it." Matthew smiled. "So, what else do you do, you know, outside of work?"

Veronica told him of her volunteer work, her tutoring of college tech students, her involvement in the local chess team, and about her outings with her two best friends. Matthew laughed at her story of the creation of her dating profile. He told her his and admitted much of the same issues that she confessed to. Dating was awkward, and meeting people was even more difficult than ever. Online dating took some of the anxiety off and allowed him to meet and greet people before meeting face-to-face.

Veronica was so happy to hear how similar they were, and after seeing Matthew's enjoyment of the food she also enjoyed and recommended to him, she was sure the date was going perfectly. They were in sync with each other — their hobbies, their jobs, their goals, their mindset... could it get any more perfect?

After dinner was finished, and the waiter cleared away their plates, Matthew offered to pay the check. Veronica said she should pay for at least some of it, but Matthew waved her off. He wanted to pay, he said.

"I want to treat you. And I'll have you know, this is the best date I've been on for quite some time."

"Me, too." Veronica smiled, her chest warming.

"I can't believe how in sync we are with each other. It's crazy, isn't it?" He laughed. "I guess it's a good thing that our friends made us set up dating profiles."

"Yeah," she mused. But she couldn't contain the happiness bubbling in her gut. It was all too perfect. Matthew, the restaurant, the food, the conversation, and for the first time in fifteen years, she was going on a first date, and that date was better than she could've ever asked for. And Matthew... she didn't want this night to end. She didn't want him to slip away, just as Parker had. It was all perfect — *they* were perfect together.

"Hey, are you alright?" he asked, eyeing her.

She brushed aside a few loose strands of hair and nodded briskly. "I'm just... thinking."

"About what? Enlighten me with that big brain of yours." He smiled teasingly.

Veronica took a deep breath and forced the words through her lips. "I think... I love you, Matthew."

Matthew's eyes widened. "What?"

She leaned forward in a rush, but he leaned away.

"I know it sounds crazy. I know we just met, but doesn't it feel right? I mean, we practically have the same career and are interested in all the same things. We're so *perfect* together. Don't you agree?"

Matthew's jaw dropped wordlessly. "Well, yeah. It's been really nice, and I'm interested in you, but we're still strangers. You can't... you can't love a complete stranger."

Veronica felt him retreating, she felt him slipping through her fingers, and she tried her very best to keep him from falling away.

"I know. I know! But I just... it all feels so right. And I just... I think you're the one for me."

In that moment, the waiter returned the check, and Matthew plucked his card from the sleeve. He stuck it into his pocket and pulled on his coat.

No... no, no, no! Veronica thought.

"I think I should go. This is... weird," Matthew said dryly.

"Matthew, no. Please don't go. Can't you see it? How perfect we are together?"

Matthew adjusted his glasses before pushing in his chair. "Maybe, but we can only really know that with time. And you just... told me you love me on the first date. Doesn't that seem at all odd to you?"

Veronica tensed, her shoulders painfully tight. "It's love at first sight."

Matthew shook his head. "For being so analytical, you're awfully romantic."

"Isn't that a good thing?"

He stared at her, his kind blue eyes now dark and cold. "Not if it's hopeless and unreasonable." He shook his head and stepped toward the door. "Have a nice night," he mumbled.

The door chimed, announcing his departure. Veronica sat there in silence, staring at the spot he abandoned until the restaurant closed, and she was asked to leave.

Matthew never contacted Veronica again after their date. So, she moved on to others. One after another, the men in her inbox dwindled. She went on five more first dates, and five separate times, she confessed her love to the men after realizing how perfect they were for her. Five separate times, the men looked at her with a mixture of shock, confusion, and pity. Five separate times, they left her there, alone, abandoned, and lovesick.

Maybe she really *was* a hopeless romantic like Matthew had said. But she didn't stop trying to find someone who loved her right back. That's how she found herself on a date with Mr. Number Seven.

Chapter Three

Rodney Hersey. His name popped up on her phone screen from one of the dating apps she used. Veronica eyed the incoming message. Did she really want to talk to a completely new man? Was she ready for yet another rejection? She stared at the notification and sighed. She swiped right to open it.

> **RODNEY**
>
> Hello, sweetheart. I hope this doesn't come off as creepy, but I matched with your profile and had to reach out. You are simply… stunning.

Veronica's cheeks burned bright red as she read the message over and over again. She clicked on his profile picture to open his page. He was thirty-four, a little older than the others she had looked at and talked to, but she didn't mind the four-year age gap. He worked as a travel agent but was very much a homebody. He enjoyed hiking, crosswords and sudoku, and cooking in his spare time. And his profile picture... Veronica stared for entirely too long at his face, taking in every detail.

He had light, fair skin and hair that looked black in the light, and pointed and poked up from his scalp in a perfectly messy attempt. His green eyes glowed in the sunlight, looking like glossy emeralds. His smile was wide and crooked, so very much like Parker's. But Rodney didn't have dimples like Parker. Instead, he had a tiny scar on the corner of his upper lip, the only blemish on his otherwise perfect face.

Veronica clicked back to her inbox and began typing a reply.

VERONICA

> Thank you. I hope this doesn't come off as creepy, but you look like a model and way out of my league.

She hit send and immediately felt regret. Had she been too forward? Had she revealed her creeping on his picture? Did she seem shallow because she only complimented his appearance? What if—?

Ding!

She eyed her phone and saw the notification for a new message. She opened it.

RODNEY

> We can both be creeps then. ;-)

She chuckled, but another message came through from him.

RODNEY

> How are you doing today, Veronica?

She typed back.

VERONICA

I'm alright. Better now. How are you, Rodney?

RODNEY

Oh, I'm just grand. Couldn't be better.

She peered at his picture again, butterflies lifting off in her gut.

RODNEY

Are you doing anything tonight, Veronica?

Her heart skipped at his usage of her name yet again. Something about hearing her name, hearing it on a man's lips, especially a man so attractive... she couldn't resist it.

VERONICA

I have no plans as of now.

She replied.
Rodney typed back quickly.

RODNEY

Dinner, then. At the Mexican place on the corner of Center and 116th. Does that sound good to you?

Veronica stared at his message. That was the restaurant she had chosen for her and Matthew's date. It was one of her favorites. But he couldn't know that, right? She scrolled up through the measly message history between them. Normally, she talked via messages to her potential dates before meeting them. Matthew and the others after, she had spoken to for at least a week before feeling comfortable enough to meet up. But this man, this gorgeous and charming man, wanted to meet her right away.

She was hesitant, as anyone might be when deciding to

meet a stranger from online in physical form. But something pulled at her, tugged at her to go, to meet him. She couldn't put a name to it, but she knew it was the right thing to do. She typed back her response.

VERONICA

Sounds perfect.

RODNEY

Great, see you then. :-)

Veronica looked at the time on the corner of her screen and found it later than expected. She rushed to shower, shave, pull out an appropriately outfit — something perfectly balanced between cute and sexy, and do her hair.

When she finally finished, it was 6:50pm. She raced downstairs and down the block to the Mexican restaurant. She crashed through the door at exactly 7:02pm, and it didn't take her long to find Rodney. He sat facing the door and looked up at her wild entrance. She smiled clumsily, expecting her tardiness and now messy appearance to put him off, but he smiled at her, his eyes gentle and bright.

"Veronica, so nice to meet you." He practically purred, his voice deliciously deep.

She sat down across from him and smoothed down her hair. "I'm so sorry I'm late. I lost track of time and couldn't get my unruly hair to work with me and... God, I'm sorry. I understand if you don't want to stay."

He raised a perfectly arched brow at her. "Do you want me to leave?"

Her eyes widened. "No! No, of course not."

"Good." He cut her short, his words ringing with authority. "Because it's okay if you were running slightly late. And it's okay if you're feeling a little flustered. Neither of those things would cause me to leave. I'm not that pretentious." He chuckled.

"Oh, well. Okay." She shuffled under the table, playing with her fingers on her lap.

Veronica suddenly found it hard to meet Rodney's bright gaze. It didn't just feel like any other person's gaze; it was hot and consuming. It felt like his eyes penetrated through her to her very core. She flushed red in the cheeks but looked up as he chuckled.

"A shy one, are we?" he teased.

Veronica's cheeks burned, but Rodney's gaze trickled down to her neck.

"I'm, um...," she cleared her throat, "so, you're a travel agent?"

Rodney smiled at her, the curl of his lips all-knowing. Up this close, she could just make out the scar on his upper lip that she remembered from his pictures. Even though he knew what she was doing, he allowed her to side track his attention from her rosy cheeks. He told her all about his job and how he enjoyed learning about different cultures and different people. And based on the information he learned, he designed unique itineraries and booked trips for others looking to get away. He figured out their needs and desires, and based on his knowledge, he created a memorable trip that catered to them.

Veronica nodded along and imagined herself on a plane to some far-off country. It would be good to travel, she thought. To get away from the city, to explore, to find herself again, and maybe, just maybe, she'd get lucky and find a sexy foreign man interested in her, too. She filed that idea away for later and smiled at Rodney.

"What do you do for a living?" he asked her.

She briefly explained her job and duties, and he seemed as fascinated by it all as she had for him.

"You're very analytical, then," he noted.

She nodded. "I always have been. But data and analytics aren't always right."

"What do you mean?"

She took a sip of her drink. "Well, I find patterns in data, and those patterns translate into some kind of conclusion. But when I take data from my own life, for example, dating — messaging guys on a dating app, meeting in person, having a great time, talking easily, meshing perfectly — all that data put together should equal something bigger. The conclusion would be that something *more* comes of it, right?"

"Right."

"And yet, when I take those next steps forward and reach for that conclusion, all the guys I talk to run away."

"What's the conclusion you've drawn?" Rodney balanced on his propped-up hand, eyeing her with sincere interest.

She swallowed, the lump returning to her throat. With her next words, this could either make or break the date. And based on past history and data, it would break it. But she had to try — she *had* to!

"Well, according to all my data, I conclude that I... love these men. I must."

"Hm." Rodney watched her. She expected rolled eyes, another man up and leaving after another failed first date. But Rodney made no move to get up. He watched her intently, that subtle, coy smile toying at his scarred lips.

"And what about me?"

"You?" She wavered.

"Do I fit into this pattern?" His eyes danced, but something darker, something hot and deep and powerful burned behind them.

"I mean, normally the data stem from all of my earlier conversations with these men. Before I met them in person. But you and I... haven't really talked much."

"So, you're stepping out of your comfort zone and analyzing new data."

Veronica eyed him, her chest tight and hot. What was happening to her? This wasn't the pattern; this wasn't even necessarily love at first sight like she had with all the others. But Rodney... he was attractive, flirty, a good listener, and genuinely interested. Should she reach toward a new conclusion?

"With the others... we talked beforehand and found similar interests. But you, you're so much different than me, Rodney."

Rodney's smile curled. "Is that bad?"

"No, just..."

"Just...?"

"New." Veronica admitted. "Unexpected. I don't really know how we would fit together."

"Don't know until you try, right?"

He took her hand in his and squeezed gently. His fingers were warm, lean, and tender. She never wanted to let them go. Rodney got it. He understood her like none of the others had. And even if he didn't fit her perfectly like a glove, even if his background and his interests were different, even if *he* was different — maybe different was what she needed.

Her chest tightened and heated as his gaze lingered. She could feel her cheeks burning again, but she ignored her shyness as she tucked a stray strand of hair behind her ear. Rodney watched her every motion. She wanted his attention on her; she never wanted to lose his gaze. And before she knew better, before she could even try to stop the words from escaping her, she blurted them out.

"Rodney, I... thank you for asking me out today, and thank you for listening. I, um, I really appreciate it."

"I'm as happy as you are to be here," he said. But as he

watched her, he tilted his head. "But that isn't what you wanted to say to me, is it?"

Veronica's gaze widened, but his lips curled into a tight smirk.

"Well, I..."

"You... what, Veronica?" he teased.

She squeezed his hand tight, and in a rush, everything came out. "I love you, Rodney. I... I know it sounds crazy, and you definitely don't fit my normal data pattern but... I just have this feeling with you and... well, I just—"

Veronica was cut short when Rodney stood from his chair, leaned over the table, and grabbed the sides of her head. He pulled her close enough to smell the mint on his breath. She shivered.

"I love you, too, Veronica," he whispered.

And then his lips crashed into hers.

They were hot and wet, and sucked impatiently at her own. She inhaled him in, basking in his scent, his taste, his presence over her. She let him take control, and he did so seamlessly. They broke apart for only a moment as he shoved money onto the table and grabbed her again to lead her outside. He pressed her up against the wall to the side of the building. She sighed and cried out impishly. Rodney took full advantage of her opened mouth, letting his tongue explore.

He pulled back after many moments and whispered in her ear. "Veronica, will you marry me?"

She paused, her swollen lips frozen in shock. He... this man — he wanted her? All to himself?

She nodded slowly at first, then faster.

"Really?" he whispered.

She pulled his face within inches of her own. "Bring me home and make me yours," she whispered.

Rodney needed no more motivation than that as he picked her up, bridal style, and threw her into a cab he hailed at the corner. She giggled at his dramatic exit, but once inside the cab, they were all over each other again. The night was a blur of sweat, moaning, intoxication, and pleasure.

It wasn't until Veronica woke up in a foreign bed the next morning, Rodney asleep at her side, that she remotely questioned what had happened. But one look at the ring on her finger, and all hesitation and denial flickered.

That was, until another woman, short, stout, and with hard features, stepped through the bedroom door. She stared hard at Veronica, still naked and wrapped up in the bed sheets.

"Your breakfast is downstairs, whenever you're ready," she said, her voice equally as thick and husky as she appeared outwardly.

Veronica watched her go in silence, the door clicking shut behind her. She stared at the solid wood before Rodney sighed out of his slumber beside her. He peeked an eye open and smiled at her.

"Hello, sweetheart. Sleep well?"

As he sat up and kissed her cheek, she felt nothing but a burning chill on her skin. She got dressed in her clothes from the night before, but her shoes were nowhere to be seen. When she asked Rodney, he said she wouldn't have to worry about wearing shoes anymore. She wavered, but he didn't react, so she followed him down two flights of steps to the first floor.

They stepped into a wide, farmhouse kitchen that she could only admire from the magazines she flipped through at the dentist. But she didn't even have a chance to admire this one because surrounding the kitchen, were four other women of varying ages, but mostly still young. They all eyed her with that same hard gaze that the first one had.

"Good morning, ladies. I hope you all slept well. Serena, thank you for the wakeup call this morning. I would have slept in until noon had you not come in." Rodney chuckled.

Serena, the woman who came into the bedroom, huffed out a forced laugh but didn't look away from her.

Rodney nibbled on a piece of toast before planting himself by her side again. He wrapped an arm around Veronica's shoulder and grinned, the crumbs of toast still dotting his stubbled chin.

"Ladies, this is Veronica. She will be joining us from now on. Veronica, meet Serena, Rachel, Nikki, and Quinn."

Veronica lifted her hand in an awkward wave, and the other women nodded silently. Serena stared at her harshly. Rachel looked younger than her with long dark hair, olive skin, and a chest many women would pay whole savings accounts for. Nikki was petite, pale as a ghost, with bright red hair that sprung off her scalp like corkscrews. She barely met Veronica's gaze. And Quinn eyed her behind glasses, one corner of which Veronica could see was broken. She was tall but unusually thin, like she might float away from the next breeze.

"Now, I must be heading off to work." Rodney glanced at a watch on his wrist. "But you ladies take care of Veronica and welcome her kindly, please."

"Wait, what—"

Rodney took her face in his hands and kissed her long and hard. When he finally came up for air, Veronica found that she couldn't get enough oxygen into her lungs.

"You be good now. I'll be home again this evening, okay?"

"But—"

Rodney kissed her forehead, not letting more words pass her lips. He made for the door and stopped at the opening.

"Welcome home, sweetheart." He gave Veronica one more tight smile, and the door clicked shut behind him, followed by six heavy locks.

Veronica stared after him in silence until Rachel touched her shoulder. She turned.

"Come on, let's get you cleaned up. Then I can show you around."

Veronica let the woman lead her to the shower, where she wordlessly cleaned her body, finding the marks and scratches all over from the night before. When she came out again, Rachel gave her a set of fresh clothes.

"But where are mine?" she asked.

Rachel pushed the thin, plaid smock into her hands. "It's better to get rid of them now. It makes it easier to move on."

"Move on... from what?"

"From your previous life."

"My... what are you talking about?"

Serena and the others stepped into the bedroom doorway.

"Your life is over, dear. You live here now," Serena said harshly.

Veronica couldn't swallow past the lump in her throat. "What does that mean?"

"You said yes to his proposal, didn't you?" Quinn chimed in.

Veronica nodded silently.

All the girls' eyes dropped like they knew too well what that meant.

"What?" Veronica asked, a well of panic rising up her throat. "What?"

"You accepted his proposal, dear. You're one of us now." At Serena's words, Veronica stiffened.

But she didn't have to ask what being "one of them" meant, because Serena wasn't the gentle talker in the household. She sat down on a chair in the corner of the bedroom and eyed Veronica. "You're married to him now. You're a Hersey wife. Just like the rest of us."

Veronica had to sit on the corner of the bed to avoid fainting.

Chapter Four

It turned out Rodney Hersey had five wives. And all five of them were trapped in this house under his orders. He came and went as he pleased for business and pleasure, but all his wives weren't permitted to leave the house under any circumstance. The only one who had was Nikki, who turned out to be shyer and more afraid than any of the others.

Nikki helped Rodney pick up groceries once a week. She went to the small local store with him, followed him quietly as he pushed the cart from aisle to aisle and made mindless, polite chit chat with other customers, and then helped him load the car and unload it once they returned to the house. She was the only one permitted to do this task with him because of her quiet, skittish nature.

Serena used to do it when she was the first wife, but after Rodney had gained more and more women in his household, she apparently went off the deep end and became wild in public. Thankfully for Rodney, people in town called her "crazy" and assumed, after her disappearance from the public eye, that Rodney had divorced her. Or so he told them.

Rachel was calmer generally, and friendlier than the

others, but she also had fiery fits. She was stubborn and strong-minded, making her impossible to bring out in public.

And Quinn — Quinn was quiet like Nikki, but she wasn't afraid or shy like her smaller, meek counterpart. Quinn was watchful, intent, and sharp, like a knife that could stab you in the back at any moment. She listened well to Rodney, as much as the others did, but Quinn always appeared deep in thought, like she was plotting something.

Veronica got along with the other four women well enough, but found it hard to empathize with them.

Why did they accept his proposal?

"I was in a hard place. My boyfriend dumped me, my parents abandoned me, I didn't have money, couldn't afford a place... Rodney showed up with a promise of love and care at the right time."

What did Rodney do to them?

"Nothing bad at first. We are expected to wait on him hand and foot, like maids. And most of the time, he's pleasant enough, mostly just creepy. But when he gets mad... that's a different story."

What did he do when he got mad?

"You don't want to know. Just don't make him get there. And if he comes home mad... stay out of his way."

Why didn't they try to get out?

"The house is locked at every entrance and exit point. All windows, doors, attic spaces, basement — and all the windows are made of some kind of unbreakable, sound proof material that's single-sided so we can't break ourselves out, and no one from the outside can see or hear us in here. There's no way *to* escape."

Why didn't Nikki say something when she was outside?

"Have you seen the girl? She's barely said two words to us, much less cry for help in public with the man himself right at her hip."

Why didn't they all overthrow him and get the key to escape? They outnumbered him; surely, they could win in a fight.

Serena shook her head sadly. "No, my dear, we wouldn't."

"Why not?" Veronica paced the kitchen back and forth, and back and forth, and back and—

"Because he has a gun."

Veronica paused. "Has he... ever used it?"

Serena swallowed, the bulge in her throat bobbing. She shook her head as her hand covered her face. Nikki stepped behind her and stroked her hunched back.

"He used his gun once," Rachel said from her perch on the kitchen island stool. "He only needed to use it once."

"What did he do?" she asked quietly.

Rachel eyed Serena before her deep voice whispered, "He shot Serena. And he killed another wife."

Veronica's breath caught in her throat. "He... he killed a woman?"

Rachel nodded slowly. "The last wife, the Number Five before you. Her name was Anna."

Serena choked on a sob, rough sniffling echoing in the silent room.

"What happened?" Veronica whispered.

Quinn chimed in then from her spot in the doorway, leaning on the frame. "Anna asked many of the same questions that you're asking, but she refused to stay here. She made a plan to escape and wanted to bring us all with her. So, she devised a plan, where we would attack Rodney upon his arrival from work, knock him out, get his keys, and then escape to the nearest house or police station to get help."

"So, what went wrong?"

"Rodney had a gun at his hip. Anna attacked from the front, and Serena attacked from behind. Rachel and I went for his legs, and Nikki hid because, well, we didn't want her to get hurt. But once we managed to get Rodney to the ground, he turned and shot blindly. It just so happened that the person in range was Anna.

"She collapsed and bled out on the floor right over there." Quinn pointed toward the front door, to which Serena's muffled cry grew louder. "We all ran from him in fear, and he came after us. But even after he rounded us up, threatened to kill us, and asked who had initiated the plan, none of us would crack. Until he turned the gun on Nikki."

"Nikki had nothing to do with the plan and had been hiding all along! He even found her hiding in the cupboard. He knew she was innocent, and he still put that stupid gun right to her head!" Rachel cried out.

Quinn hushed her, but Rachel was fuming.

"He threatened to kill Nikki if we didn't talk," Quinn conceded. "He was willing to kill an innocent woman whom he had stolen and hid away himself to begin with, all so we would be fearful enough to give him what he wanted."

Veronica glanced at Nikki, who had quiet tears running down her cheeks.

"But he already killed Anna. Wasn't that enough? You said she was the one who plotted the attack in the first place."

Serena lifted her head then, her eyes bloodshot and angry in the dim light coming in through the windows. "He killed Anna accidentally, but I don't think he ever thought twice about it. But Nikki, dear, sweet little Nikki had done nothing wrong and, still, he raised his weapon at her. That was a choice, one he was willing to make. So, we told him that I helped Anna plan the attack."

Veronica's eyes widened. "Did you?"

Serena's hard gaze didn't waver. "In a way, yes. In others, no. But I wasn't about to let that man kill another innocent woman just because he could."

"So, he... he shot you for it?"

Serena pulled down one of her stockings to show the

scarred hole in her calf. It was twisted and red and angry, even after all this time. Veronica's jaw tightened at the sight of it.

"Shot me in the leg. It wouldn't kill me, but it would make it so I couldn't run and couldn't escape even if I tried."

The room fell silent as Serena rolled her stocking up again. The tension was so thick that one could cut it with a knife. Veronica herself was shaking with a mixture of fear, anger, anxiety, and utter, uncontained hatred. She had known Rodney Hersey the shortest amount of time, but even then, the entire blissful night she had spent with him felt like a disgusting lie.

This man who had flirted with her, charmed her, reasoned and delighted her, made her feel noticed and loved—

He was a liar, a cold-blooded killer, an abuser, a manipulator, and psychotic if he thought he could keep her trapped here for the remainder of her days.

Veronica eyed Nikki, huddled around Serena, who held the fragile girl's hand with a thick, heavy grip of her own. Rachel, who sat hunched and fuming on the bar stool, tense with angry energy. And Quinn, who watched from a distance, cold, hard, and calculating, but unrelenting. Veronica took a deep, steadying breath.

"We should try to escape."

All the women looked up at her like she was crazy.

"Weren't you just listening? We just told you a whole extended story of why we *can't* escape," Quinn snapped.

"I *was* listening. Were you? Because all I hear and see are four strong women who have been beaten down, manipulated, and abused by Rodney Hersey. And while they made a stand, it failed. So, what? You're just going to give up? You're just going to live out the rest of your days in this house calling yourselves his 'wives' with no argument, no fight of your own?"

"He'll kill us all if we try to escape again, Veronica. It's not reasonable." Rachel scowled.

But Veronica wasn't so sure. "No. You just haven't studied him enough. You haven't collected enough data. You have to find the pattern first, and then build a conclusion."

The four of them looked at her like she had three heads. She sighed.

"We have to figure out his schedule, his habits, his preferences, the exact timing of his actions, and the choices he'll make when offered them. Only then can we make a foolproof plan. One that will grant us all our freedom and won't get anyone else hurt."

Rachel and Quinn eyed her skeptically. Nikki watched on in stunned silence, but it was Serena, with the hole in her leg, who stood up. She huffed, leaning awkwardly to one side because of her wound. But that didn't stop her from looking strong and certain as she met Veronica's gaze.

"It's time. We can't let him hold us down with fear anymore." Nikki nodded ever so slightly, and the other two, maybe out of surprise after seeing Nikki's reaction, nodded, too. "Tell us what we need to do."

Chapter Five

Veronica put the plan in action after a week of gathering data. With the help of the four other women, they tracked Rodney's schedule to the minute. They gathered his preferences in regards to women, situations, and entertainment. They figured out who he talked to and trusted more, and who could distract him if needed. They discerned from Nikki's memory from going to the grocery store how to get there, and figured it would be a good enough place as any to get help. They talked about his weaknesses, his blind spots, and after a week of digging and relentless flirting and nights in bed with all of them, they discovered his hiding place.

In the drawer of his nightstand. He put his watch in there every night and closed the door. After some spying in the middle of the night, Rachel thought he only put the watch there and nothing more. It appeared mostly empty.

But then Quinn found the lever above the top lip of the opening; there was a tab. When pushed to the side, a compartment opened up at the drawer's bottom. And inside, there were two keys. One was for the safe in the bedroom, which once they opened it, they found cash and ammo for his handgun. The other key was for the bedroom, need he ever lock it, which he hadn't, the women told Veronica, except for right after Anna's death. He had dragged her body into the bedroom and locked it up for two days. After he reopened it, Anna's body was gone, and in its place, were ten small garbage bags, reeking of something rotten and foul.

The women didn't ask any questions; they couldn't in fear of what the answer might be. But they knew; it was unavoidable with the stench that lingered for weeks after.

From this information, they created a plan together, and that evening, when Rodney returned home at exactly 6:02pm as planned, they put it into action.

Serena made them all dinner and had it prepared and ready on the table for when he showed up. He sat down with a smile and greeted them all like any other day.

"How are my ladies doing?"

They all smiled tightly, fingers fidgeting on their laps, and forks scraping food across their mostly full plates. But Rodney paid no mind. He talked about his day at work and complained about his boss, who apparently babied him "like the royal asshole he was." Babied him — how unfortunate for him, truly.

But as he talked, they all gave each other flickering gazes. It was almost time. He would be finished eating, and his plate needed to be cleared in three minutes. And it was.

He would then go to the living area and watch a documentary on something only he was interested in for an hour and a half. Rachel would offer him a drink, whiskey with a splash of Coke, just as he liked. But Serena's foul cooking, in addition to the liquor, wouldn't sit well in his stomach. But he showed no sign of it during the movie. It was still early though.

Then he would use the toilet, brush his teeth, and kiss all

of them goodnight before choosing one to go to bed with him that night. He chose Veronica, her flirtiness during dinner and sensual touching during the movie made her certain that she'd be picked.

He brought her into the bedroom. He laid her back onto the mattress. She curled around him with all the grace and sexual attraction she could muster, all while the plan burned in her mind, and the memory of Anna and Serena's injuries made her blood boil.

"Take this big thing off; it's poking me in all the wrong places." She pouted, tugging at his watch. He chuckled before sliding it off and into the nightstand.

She kissed him hotly, not giving him time to breathe. But when he finally pulled back for air, he looked pale.

"I don't feel so well, sweetheart. Give me a moment." And with that, he ran off to the bathroom, locked the door, and she could hear him emptying the contents of his stomach into the bowl.

Veronica made her move. She wedged the chair from the corner under the door knob and moved to the nightstand. She yanked open the drawer and felt for the tab. It flicked under pressure, and the compartment opened up. She grabbed the safe key and the room key but again, there were only two keys. She hoped he would put the front door key in the same compartment, but it wasn't there. She grunted in frustration and heard the toilet flush once.

In a hurry, she grabbed his watch, too, and closed the nightstand. She wanted to get the money from the safe, or perhaps the ammo, so he wouldn't have any for his gun. She hoped his gun might be in there, too, but he must still have it on his body, hidden somewhere under his clothes.

She ran out the door as she heard the sink turn off. The door handle jiggled.

"Veronica? I think the lock is jammed. Veronica? Are you there?" he called.

Veronica slammed the bedroom door shut behind her and lock it in place, just as she heard kicking and bashing from inside. She flew down the hall and down the stairs, where the others waited.

"Hurry!" Rachel called.

She threw herself down the last few steps and landed in a huffing heap in Serena's arms.

"He didn't put the key in the compartment. There's no key to the front door."

"Then how are we supposed to get out?" Rachel yelled. "And why do you have his watch?"

"He wears it constantly, and keeps it with his other hidden things. I thought it might be important!" Veronica yelled, panic rising in her throat as a roar echoed from upstairs.

"Veronica!" Rodney's deep voice radiated downstairs like a vicious beast on the loose. She shivered. They had to get out; they had to go... *now!*

Nikki watched them all silently, bouncing on the balls of her feet. But Quinn grabbed the watch from her hands.

"You're right. He's always wearing it. And it seems odd that he'd keep it alongside his keys. Maybe..." She turned it around and around in her hands.

"Talk, Quinn!"

"I'm looking... ah!"

She flicked a cap open and pressed a small button, and out popped a piece of thin metal. Veronica pulled it out slowly and, sure enough, it was a key. She slid it into the lock and slowly, too slowly, each lock clicked open one by one. A sigh of relief escaped her, but too soon.

The door upstairs slammed open, crashing against the wall, and angry footsteps pounded on the steps.

Nikki cried out, "he's coming!"

They all turned and faced the beast at the stair landing. He fumed, his once charming and beautiful features warping with rage.

"You! After everything I've done for you, you're going to try and escape again? Good luck with that." He gritted out, pulling his gun from his waistband.

Veronica and the others shrieked, ducking behind the half wall by the door. Only Serena stood firm.

"Your time is over, Rodney. Let us go."

Rodney laughed, deep, dark, and horrendously.

"You think I'd do that? Just like that?"

"You have no other choice. You let us all go now in peace, or the other girls will escape while I take you down with me."

Rodney stopped at the bottom of the landing, gun still poised. "You think you can take me on after what I did to you?" He huffed.

But Serena was prepared to fight this time. She hurled for his head and dodged the angle of his gun. He shot into the far wall, and the other four women screamed, but Serena wasn't going to let him hurt any of them this time. She tackled him to the ground and threw away his gun. He fought back, pushing against her weight, but Serena held firm.

"Go!" she called over her shoulder. "Get out of here!"

They all ran to the door as Rodney cried out in rage, but none of them could walk through the open door without their friend.

"We can't go without you, Serena!" Rachel cried.

Quinn teared up, sniffling and shaking like Veronica had never seen before. But likewise, it was Nikki who surprised them all and pushed them through. She nodded at Serena.

"Thank you, Serena. I'll get you help; just hold on!"

Serena smiled sadly as the four women ran into the darkness. They ran down empty streets and hurdled over curbs and hills, the wind on their faces stinging like a cold ocean. They ran and ran until they reached the grocery store, and then they ran inside. They called for help, they screamed for help, and within minutes, the employees called the cops, soothed the women in a back room where they insisted they'd hide, and then the police showed up.

The End

Three Little Words

Three Dates

TROUBLED GIRLS FIND LOVE

Three
Dates

Amelia Ainsworth wasn't looking for an arranged marriage, but she had finally given in to her aunt's pleas to set her up on a date with what Evelyne called "the perfect match." All she knows about Alistair is that he's the son of her friend, Merlyn, and a smart, kind-hearted young man in medical school.

And it certainly doesn't hurt that he's both handsome and charming.

He's her date for three nights. That's the deal. Three dates set up by her aunt as her dying wish. The first one goes smoothly. But it's like being on a set, playing a part. Doing what's expected of them.

However, by date number three, she finds herself running away from him and into the arms of another man.

And now Amelia is starting to regret having made that decision.

Is it too late to turn back?

Can she apologize for her mistake and get Alistair to forgive her?

Or did she just push away the potential love of her life forever?

Chapter One

"Ow! What the fuck?" Amelia Ainsworth hissed loudly as she sprung her head up from in between her arms. She looked over at her best friend, Melody Kim, who was glaring at her as if something bad were going to happen soon... very, very soon.

"I see you're using my class as your own personal naptime again, Ms. Ainsworth."

Amelia looked up, just to find the entire lecture hall of eighty plus students staring at her, some smirking, many chuckling. Her physics professor, Professor Ambone, stood at the front with his arms crossed over his chest.

"S-Sorry," she apologized half-heartedly. "I was up late last night."

"That's...," Ambone paused to count his fingers, "the thirteenth time this month. Either you need a doctor to cure that problematic narcolepsy of yours, or I suggest you pull yourself together to avoid failing my class."

More chuckles echoed throughout the lecture hall, and Amelia clenched her fists together, her nails digging deep into her skin.

"Y-Yes, sir," she mumbled.

"I sure hope so, Ms. Ainsworth. And oh, you might want to clean up your face a bit. You got some dribble beginning to crust on the side of your mouth." He then turned to the rest of the class. "Class dismissed. And don't forget the final exam the week after spring break. I'm sure you've all been studying diligently."

"Ugh," Amelia groaned, shoving her books into her bag.

"Up all night swiping again?" Melody asked as she followed her friend out the double doors.

"Huh? What gave it away?"

"Come on, Lia, you only ever drool when you're thinking about guys. Who is it this time?"

"Lucas Liard. I even super liked him, too. And still, not of hint of interest in return. Blonde, 6'2, abs like a god, dazzling blue eyes, a smile that literally drenches me... *and* he likes foie gras! Do you know how difficult it is to fine someone, not just a guy, who likes foie gras? I mean, it's like we're a match made in Heaven, like God sat on his little throne up in the sky and stitched us together!" Amelia exclaimed and threw her hands up in the air, her bag dangling off her right shoulder.

"Bleh! Disgusting! I don't know how you eat that. One sniff, and I wanna gag."

"But, Mel, aren't Lucas and I just *perfect* for each other?! Just meant to be?"

"Yeah, perfect in a world of delusion. He hasn't even liked you back. Do you know anything about him beyond what his profile says?"

"Duh! He goes to Harper College, is on the lacrosse team, and has two sisters."

Melody rolled her eyes.

"What?"

"I meant, anything *other* than what you found stalking his social media."

"Well... no, not yet. But it's still early on in our relationship. There's plenty to learn about each other!"

Melody blinked and continued to stare at her friend. "You okay?"

That's when Amelia broke down and started to wail. "Why is it that all the good ones never like me back? Sixteen months! It's been exactly sixteen months and two days since David left me, and I *still* can't find another boyfriend!"

"Maybe you just need a longer break. You know, Lia, it's good to just be alone sometime." Melody adjusted the strap of her bag on her shoulder, checking her phone for the time. "Can we go get lunch now? I'm starving."

But Amelia ignored her question. "You have Kyle. He adores you so much that he'll literally kiss your feet. You don't know how difficult it is for those who are still single."

Her patience weakening, Melody raised her tone. "Well, Lia, I don't know what to tell you. Your standards are too damn high, and you try to date people who are completely out of your league! Let's face it, we're both sevens at best. Of course, you're gonna fall if you go chasing after a ten! Maybe it's time you find another seven."

"Lower my standards? Are you serious? David was a nine. It's either I go higher than that, or I'm staying single for the rest of my life."

Melody shrugged her shoulders and started walking away. "Guess you're staying single forever. I'm getting pizza."

LATER THAT NIGHT, Amelia leaned against her pillow on her bed and pulled up the app. According to her, there isn't a better feeling in the world than changing into her cozy robe, climbing under her sheets, and scrolling through her phone.

"Nerd. Nerd. Gap tooth. Ugly. Ugly. Gross. Ew. Ugly.

Short. Ugly. Ugh! Why is this so hard?!" She'd been on her phone for the past two hours, scrolling nonstop, guy after guy, and not a single match. She paused and swiped the app away, pulling up Lucas' social media profile, smiling as if his smile on one of his pictures were smiling back at her, leaning in to kiss her phone gently. "It's been almost a full day since I super liked you. Why are you ignoring me?!"

And suddenly, her phone started to ring. Her mother.

"Hey, Mom, what's up?"

"Hi, honey, how's school treating you? You doing okay? I can't wait to see my little girl's name on the Dean's List."

"Aw, come on, Mom. College is supposed to be about having fun, finding myself. You can't seriously expect me to study all the time."

"But your brother—"

"I'm not like Jason, okay? He's a nerd! His nose is always shoved inside a book that I bet he has no life!"

"Amelia!"

"Sorry, I get that you want me to go to med school like him, but that's not me, Mom. Let me make my own decisions for once." There was a loud sigh on the other line. *"What is it, Mom? Everything okay?"*

"What? Oh, yes, everything's great, dear. Listen, can you come home tomorrow night? I know you're on spring break next week, and I was thinking you could spend a few days at home, with your family. Your Aunt Evelyne's visiting Friday night before going on her business trip, and it'll be good for us to all have dinner together."

Amelia looked over at her calendar. She hated visiting home, particularly because she always got compared to Jason whenever she's around her family. But she hadn't been in over five months, and it wasn't like she had anything else planned for the next upcoming days. Honestly, she'd hoped to spend all of spring break swiping through more potential suitors.

Every day she isn't using the app means another day spent without her new boyfriend.

"Fine, I'll drive back tomorrow night."

"Wonderful! I'll even make your favorite, pot roast and garlic baked potatoes. I love you, honey."

"Love you too, Mom."

When she hung up, Amelia reached under her dorm bed and grabbed a bag of family-sized sour cream and onion chips along with a beer.

"It's going to be a long night," she whispered and pulled up the app.

<h1 style="text-align:center">Chapter Two</h1>

"Can I get an iced coffee, please? Extra-large?" Amelia asked the freckled-faced teenager at the counter of the university's coffee shop. She barely had the strength to stay awake in English Lit, and now she had to drive two and half hours back home to her parents.

"I really, really don't think you're in the condition to drive home, Lia. What if you pass out on the wheel?" Melody asked as she grabbed her own drink from the teenager, a medium matcha green latte with extra foam.

"No, I canceled on them the past three times. I can't do it again."

"Why not just go home tomorrow? I mean, you *do* have an entire week to spend with them," Melody suggested and took a sip from her cup.

But Amelia shook her head. "Can't do that, either. My Aunt Evelyne is coming over tonight before leaving town for a few days. My family already sees me as a disappointment. The least I could do is show up for dinner."

"Lia, you're a mess, you know that?"

Amelia laughed and reached over to grab her coffee. "I sure

do, but a *hot* mess." Then she paused. "Are you sure you don't wanna come spend spring break with my family? It beats sitting in your dorm all by yourself."

Melody nodded. "Yeah, it's my fault, anyway. I forgot to remind my parents about spring break before they booked their flight to Puerto Rico. But it's all good. Kyle's coming to visit for a few days. At least, I'll have him to keep me company. Besides, I should really study for that physics final if I want to make the Dean's List this semester."

"Ugh, not you, too."

"What do you mean?"

"My mom went on and on last night about the fucking Dean's List, and how I should be more like my brother, and I'm just so tired of hearing about it!" She took a sip of her coffee. "Why can't I just do what I want? Live my own life."

"You mean fawning over boys and drooling in class?" Melody teased.

A slight smile drew over Amelia's face. "Oh, shut up!" And she laughed.

"So, how'd your search go last night? Did Lucas get back to you?" Melody changed the subject as they walked over to a vacant table. The coffee shop was much emptier than usual, as most of the students had already left for their break.

Amelia pulled out her phone to check if there were any new messages. Nothing. "I think he's playing hard to get."

"I think he's playing not interested." Melody burst into laughter and tilted her head back.

"That's not funny! I truly believe that Lucas Liard is the man for me. He just hasn't realized it yet. He'll come around soon, trust me."

"If you say so."

AN HOUR LATER, Amelia said farewell to her friend and walked toward the parking garage with her suitcase. She knew she didn't need much, as her room back home still had most of her things, but she didn't want to be caught in a situation where she didn't have her loyal stilettos or her sexy black dress with her.

She stepped into her car and scouted the area near her school for somewhere that was still open. The three cups of caffeine today weren't nearly enough to balance out her two hours of sleep.

"Closed. Closed. Closed," she read sign after sign out loud as she rounded each corner. "The perk of living in the middle of nowhere truly is that everything closes before seven."

A few minutes later, she spotted a gas station. Not the cleanest, but it'll do for a quick stop. She quickly pulled into a spot and walked inside, heading back toward the refrigerated section of the store. When she reached in to pull out a can of energy drink, she heard a deep voice call out her name.

"Amelia? Amelia, is that you?"

Amelia spun around and found herself staring at a lanky man around her age whom she'd never seen before. He had rounded red glasses over his eyes, messy light brown hair, and wore a long sleeve tee that looked way too oversized for him.

"Uhm, yeah... Do I know you?" she asked, backing away slightly in hopes that he'd get the hint.

"No, but you should. I'm Patrick. I super liked you on Hooked three days ago, and I never heard back from you."

Hooked, Amelia thought. *That's my app.* "Oh... uhm... yeah... sorry, I've... been super busy lately. Haven't been on the app much." *Ugh, I wanted Lucas, and instead, this freak shows up?*

"Bummer, that sucks. Well, we're both here now! What do you say we go out and grab a drink? And then maybe back to my place for some R&R?"

A small stream of bile rose in her throat, and she quickly forced herself to push it back down. "I can't, sorry. I'm actually on my way home for spring break. I'm sure you know how parents can be when you're late." *I never thought I'd be so grateful to go home.*

"Well, do you wanna swap numbers at least? That way, we can chat during break, and then hang out when you get back? There's this new arcade near here that I've been dying to go to. What do you say we make it our first date?"

Amelia felt her heart bleeding inside her chest. *Why won't this kid just go away? There's a reason I never responded to him. I don't like him. I don't like you!* But she couldn't say that to him, especially not to his face. Confrontation had always been her Achilles' heel, and she just wanted to get the hell out of there as soon as possible.

"I... I have to go. I'll message you back. But I really have to run," she stammered.

"Just quickly swap numbers. What if I don't see you again?" He began following her.

Then that surely wouldn't be the worst thing in the world. "I'll message you," she stammered again.

She spun around on her heel and quickly made her way toward the front door.

"Hey, what about your drink?" Patrick called out after her.

I'd rather risk my chance passing out at the wheel than stay another minute around this loser. "Don't need it anymore. Thanks!" And she pushed her way out the door, sprinting to her car and driving away before he had a chance to catch up to her. Her heart was beating fast, definitely not tired anymore, and she fumbled with her phone to dial Melody's number, putting her on speaker while she continued to drive.

"Lia? Aren't you heading down to your parents?"

"I was—am. Driving as we speak. You won't *believe* what just happened to me."

"Hold on, Lia. Kyle's on hold on the other line. I'll let him know I'll call him back."

Melody had been Amelia's friend ever since Freshman orientation. They met while they were on the same team together during a team-building exercise, and they instantly bonded, becoming the best of friends and sharing all their secrets with each other. So much so that Melody would immediately know when Amelia was about to enter one of her long rants.

"Alright, I'm back." Amelia heard on the other line. "What's up?"

"I was just at a gas station, trying to get an energy drink, when some loser walked up to me and asked me out, pressured me to give him my number. He said he super liked me on Hooked and, for some reason, the freak assumed that we *have* to go out. I had to fucking run out of there like my life depended on it! Didn't even get my drink. Can you believe the audacity of that guy? Coming up to me like that and demanding a date?"

"Well...," Melody began. "Was he at least cute?"

"If he was, do you really think I'll be on the phone with you right now? Calling him a loser?" Amelia could almost hear her friend shrug. She knew her all too well. "What?" she asked.

"Remind you of anyone?" Melody asked, her voice sounding smug.

"No, should it?"

"Two words, Lia. Lucas Liard."

Amelia shook her head. "No, no! This is nothing like my situation with Lucas. *I'm* not a four-eyed freak with a shirt that's too big for me. It's completely different! I'm not a loser!"

"Then why hasn't Lucas messaged you back? What if *you* were to approach *him* suddenly out in public? You don't think he'd run away, just like you did?"

"No! Maybe... possibly. Shit, I *am* a four-eyed freak with a shirt that's too big for me, aren't I?" Amelia asked, her voice cracking at the realization.

"Sounds like it to me."

Amelia fell silent, tears welling in her eyes. How could she have been so foolish, obsessing over some stranger who didn't even care about her enough to say hi?

"You okay, Lia?" Melody asked when she realized no one was answering her.

Amelia sniffled. "Yeah, yeah, I'm fine."

"Hey, don't worry about any of that, okay? Take a few days off from the dating life. Spend some quality time with your family. I'm sure they'll appreciate it."

Probably the sanest thing Amelia had heard all day. "You have a point. Thanks, Mel."

"Drive safe!"

NEARLY THREE HOURS LATER, Amelia pulled into the driveway of her childhood home. She could see her Aunt Evelyne's bright purple jeep from a block away. Her aunt was never one to keep things subtle. She was always the loudest, flashiest, and always wanted to be the center of attention, the complete opposite of her younger sister, Amelia's mother. She loved her aunt, as much as she loved the rest of her family, but there's just something about being around her for an extended period of time that made her want to rip out all her hair, strand by strand.

Amelia reached into her pocket to fish out her keys when she reached the front door. She couldn't remember the last time she even used them, surprised that her dad hadn't changed the lock. Bracing herself for endless hugs and kisses when she walked in, she, instead, found herself face-to-face with a tall, brunette man with radiant green eyes and broad shoulders.

"Hello, you must be Amelia. My name's Alistair. Alistair Haynes," he greeted her with a dazzling smile and sparkling white teeth.

"Hi...? Uhm, I'm sorry, but am I in the right house? I could've sworn—"

"Amelia, darling! There you are!" Aunt Evelyne suddenly danced out of the kitchen wearing a floral print apron that nearly blinded her eyes. "So nice to see your beautiful face again!"

"Hey, Aunt Evelyne," Amelia murmured, slightly heaving, when she aggressively pulled her into a hug.

"I see you met Alistair. He'll be joining us tonight for dinner." Amelia looked up at her aunt and saw her grinning from ear to ear, shifting her head back and forth between this man and Amelia herself.

"Am I missing something here? Who is he?" Amelia demanded from her aunt. Then she turned back to Alistair. "Sorry to be rude," then she turned back to her aunt, "but am I supposed to know him?"

Aunt Evelyne smiled. "You will soon enough, dear. You will soon enough."

As ominous as that sounded, Amelia barely had time to register what she'd meant before her mom popped her head out from the kitchen and announced, "Dinner's ready!"

"After you." Alistair gestured to Amelia and followed behind.

Quite the gentleman. I wonder what circus he came from.

Amelia's father carved out a heaping portion of pot roast for everyone when they arrived into the dining room, with only two seats left for Alistair and Amelia... right next to each other. *Something smells fishy*, Amelia thought. *And it's not just Aunt Evelyne's pits.*

Dinner was quiet at the start, with her mother starting mundane conversations about the same three topics she always conversed about: work, Jason, and how Amelia should strive to be more like Jason. By this point, she'd learned to just tune her out, focus on the potatoes in front of her while she babbled on and on.

"Amelia? Amelia!"

Amelia popped her eyes wide at the voice yelling at her. It was her mother, standing at her spot with her hands on her hips.

"What is it?" Amelia asked.

"Your Aunt Evelyne has a special announcement." She looked over to where Aunt Evelyne was seated, as did everyone else.

"Amelia, darling, you must be dying to know why this handsome young man here has decided to grace us with his presence and join us for dinner tonight," she began.

"I guess?"

"Well, truth is, I have found you a potential new husband, Alistair Haynes."

"What?!" Amelia jumped up from her seat, pushing her chair back far behind her. She shook her head, refusing to believe what she had just heard. *A husband?* "Are you insane?! I'm only twenty-one! I haven't even graduated yet. I still have my whole fucking life ahead of me, and you're already selling me off to some dude I've only just met?"

"Amelia!" Her mother hissed. "Be respectful!"

"I'm sorry if I'm intruding," Alistair began to say to Amelia, "but I was under the impression that you'd already been informed of this situation."

She crossed her arms. "Well, I haven't. Someone care to explain it to me?"

Aunt Evelyne cleared her throat loudly and began to explain. "You see, my darling Amelia. For years, I've seen you go from boy to boy, being used by people who don't deserve you. It pains me greatly to see you wear your heart on your sleeve, just to have it broken over and over again. You deserve someone better, my dear. You deserve a man." She gestured her head toward the man beside Amelia. "Alistair here, is the son of a friend of mine, Merlyn. I met him just last week when Merlyn invited me over for some tea and biscuits, and to catch up on each other's lives. But enough about me. Alistair is a wonderful young man, smart, kind-hearted, and one day, will become a very respectable doctor. He's in medical school, you know?"

Amelia simply rolled her eyes. Just the thought of being around another doctor, who'll do nothing but show her up, was enough to make her lose interest already.

"And what if I say no?" Amelia bluntly asked.

"Amelia! Can I speak to you alone in the kitchen, please?" her mother suddenly interjected.

Probably to yell at me again, Amelia thought. Nevertheless, she pushed back her chair and followed her mother into the next room, the lingering smell of pot roast making its way into her nostrils and making her stomach growl.

"What is it?" she asked.

"I need you to stop being so rude to your Aunt Evelyne."

"Why? She's trying to pawn me off to some guy I don't even know, and *I'm* the one who needs to be respectful?"

"Yes." Her mother nodded.

"No! I refuse! It's my life, not hers!"

"Amelia, please, listen to me. I didn't want to have to tell you this, not yet anyway, but your Aunt Evelyne is very, very sick. She's only sixty-two, but she's been diagnosed with stage four Leukemia, and she doesn't have much time left. Her only wish is to see that you don't live the rest of your life unhappy. She loves you; she only wants what's best for you."

"Dying? Aunt Evelyne?" Amelia's jaw dropped open in shock. She couldn't believe what she was hearing. What was supposed to be a relatively decent family dinner turned into something much darker, and she was stuck in the middle of it.

"Yes, honey. So, please, even if you decide that you don't want to marry Alistair, just go out with him, for your aunt's sake."

"Just one date?" Amelia asked, her tone much quieter, her lips trembling.

"Three. Your Aunt Evelyne is a very superstitious woman, and she believes that it'll take at least three dates with Alistair before you're able to decide whether you like him or not."

"Just three? You sure?"

"Positive. Just three dates, and if you decide you never want to see him again, then we won't fight you on it, and you can go back to living life as you want. But, please, honey, humor your Aunt Evelyne. She worked so hard to arrange this."

Amelia huffed. She still hated the idea of being set up, but three dates were hardly a chore for her dying aunt. Besides, how bad could it be? She peeked out into the dining room and saw Alistair smiling back at her, waving. And it certainly didn't hurt that he was a gift to the eyes.

After calming herself down and pushing back in her tears, Amelia smoothed down her frayed hair and made her way back in to join the rest of her family. Without looking at anyone else, she walked straight up to her Aunt Evelyne and said, "Okay, Aunt Evelyne. I will go out with Alistair."

Chapter Three

"OMG, Lia. I can't believe you're going out on an arranged date!" Melody screamed over the phone as Amelia sat in front of vanity to put on her lipstick. "This is so unlike you!"

"Ugh, don't remind me. And it's not like I really have a choice. I have to do this for my Aunt Evelyne. It's the least I could do."

"Yeah, sorry about your aunt, man. That's rough. I don't know what I'd do if I were in your shoes."

Amelia chuckled. "Sit in front of a mirror and plaster lipstick all over yourself like a doll?"

Melody joined in. "Yeah, probably. So, tell me about this guy. He cute?"

"Eh, he's not Lucas Liard, but he's not the worst looking guy in the world. Green eyes, dark hair, broad shoulders—" Amelia began.

"Oh, sounds sexy!" Melody interrupted.

"Really, Mel?"

"What? You know I'm a sucker for green eyes. Why else do you think I'm with Kyle?" Melody exclaimed.

"Uhm... because he treats you like a queen?"

"Nah, definitely the green eyes," Melody teased.

"Amelia, honey! Alistair's here!" Amelia heard her mother call up from downstairs.

"Shit, Mel, I gotta go. He's here, and I'm still in my bra." Amelia leaned in closer to her phone, ready to hang up.

"Just go like that. I'm sure he'll love it even more."

"Oh, shut up." Amelia laughed. "Alright, I gotta go."

"Call me after! I wanna know how it went."

Amelia quickly agreed and hung up. She then finished putting on the rest of her face and rushed into her closet. She looked through the racks, nothing but old T-shirts and ripped jeans. It wasn't like she'd been very keen on impressing the guy, but she couldn't show up looking like she'd just roughed it up with the boys when he was probably decked out in a suit. She could at least *make* an effort to look halfway decent.

"Amelia!" her mother called up again, her voice beginning to grow impatient.

"I'm coming!" she shouted back. "I *could* wear the black dress I brought home, but that might give him the wrong idea."

She rummaged quicker through her racks of clothes and eventually found a floral skirt that extended down to her knees, and threw on a white blouse that she hadn't worn since her cousin's wedding. After shoving her feet into a pair of heels that tore at her ankles, she walked over to look at herself in the mirror.

"Well, I hope Alistair likes going out with grannies," she mumbled.

When she made her way downstairs, Alistair was sitting on the couch with her Aunt Evelyne, sipping on some tea and enjoying her mother's famous coffee cake.

"Don't fill yourself up too much," Amelia joked, and he looked up at her.

"Wow, Amelia." Alistair smiled and stood up to greet her with a light hug. "You look amazing."

"Seriously?" She stepped back and raised a brow. "You sure I don't look like I belong in a nursing home?"

He burst out in laughter. "Not at all. I think you look stunning."

"Aw, darling! Look at you! Beautiful as the day you were born!" Aunt Evelyne stood up from where she was sitting and stumbled over to hug her niece.

"No, no, Aunt Evelyne. You stay there," Amelia called back. She rushed over to her aunt and slowly sat her back down onto the couch. "You're in no condition to be walking around unnecessarily like this."

"Oh, don't mind me," her aunt replied. "I'm just so happy that my little Amelia is finally going on a date with a decent man. Besides, I should be heading out soon for my trip."

"And they better get going if they don't want to be late." Amelia's father stepped into the living room to cut himself a slice of coffee cake. He took a bite and closed his eyes. "Mm, your mother truly makes the best."

Alistair took Amelia's hand and smiled down at her, his pearly whites shining beneath the warm living room light. "Shall we?" he asked.

"Wait! Before you go," her mother called out, running into the living room, "let me just grab a picture of you two. Something to remember this night by."

"Come on, Mom—" Amelia began.

"I'm sure the restaurant won't mind if we're a few minutes late," Alistair assured her.

Seven pictures later, Amelia finally found herself walking to Alistair's car, a sleek black Porsche, definitely a gem in the eyes of her parents.

"Sorry about all that, by the way," Amelia apologized. "My family can be a bit... much."

Alistair laughed. "No worries. I get it. Mine are pretty much the same. The difference is, you haven't met them yet."

"So, where are we going, anyway?"

"Your aunt made us a reservation at this swanky French restaurant in town. Honestly, I didn't even know it existed until she gave me the address. But it's right by the school on Main. I must've passed it hundreds of times before and just never noticed."

"Let me guess, it's looks like a hole in the wall on the outside, but once you walk in, you magically get transformed into a new world of luxury and royalty?" Amelia asked snidely.

"Something like that." He pulled out his phone. "Here, look. If I zoom in, see that tiny white building?" He was leaning in so close that Amelia could smell the scent of cologne on him. Old spice with a hint of vanilla. He smelled so good that she didn't want to pull away, even when he closed his phone and started the ignition.

A thirty-minute drive later, Alistair pulled into a cramped parking lot behind the same tiny white building she'd seen on his phone. It wasn't much, barely enough to fit three cars, but he managed to make it work.

"Ready?" he asked, and Amelia nodded, reaching her hand out to open the door. "Whoa, whoa, whoa. Stay there." He quickly got out from the driver's seat and jogged over to the passenger side, where he gracefully opened the door and bowed as he said, "A gentleman *always* opens the door for his lady."

Amelia smiled, unsure of whether it's a smile of adoration or cringe. Even so, it was the nicest thing anyone had done for her in a long time. The most gentleman-like thing David had ever done for her was not call her fat when she'd asked.

Just like in the picture, Maison Blanc looked like nothing more than a run-down block on the outside.

"Are you sure we're at the right place?" Amelia asked Alistair, who looked down at her with a smile and grabbed her hand.

"Positive," he said.

His warm touch made her heart skip a beat and her body shiver. She didn't know what she was feeling. Alistair was the complete opposite of the type of men she'd normally fall for. She liked bad boys, like Lucas and David. Alistair's demeanor, his kind and gentle personality, odd for Amelia to start fawning over. But she didn't pull her hand away. She couldn't. She had to at least try and enjoy the date, for her Aunt Evelyne's sake, anyway.

And when they walked inside, she felt like she'd been transformed into an entirely new world. Shiny chandeliers strung along the ceiling. Velvet curtains lined the walls and windows. And every waiter and waitress inside the restaurant were dressed in black tie attire, looking even better than Alistair and herself.

"Wow, this is fancy," Amelia whispered.

"Yeah, really is. Your aunt really knows how to go all out," Alistair whispered back.

"Good evening, sir, madam," the maître d' walked up to them and greeted. "Dinner for two tonight?"

Alistair nodded, grasping onto her hand a little harder. "Correct. Reservation under Ainsworth?"

The maître d' paused to flip through the thick book that laid in front of him. Seconds later, his head popped back up, and he said, "Ah, here it is. You're here for the lover's special!"

"Lover's special?" Amelia asked. "What's that?"

"Ah, madam, the lover's special is a very special course, the very best that Maison Blanc has to offer. Twelve courses, plus the finest of wines and the most decadent of desserts."

"Sounds fantastic," Alistair exclaimed. "I—we can't wait."

"Wonderful! Right this way."

The maître d' led the two of them through the small

crowded restaurant to a candlelit booth near the back. Amelia slid in first while Alistair slid in behind her, leaving a small gap between the two of them to avoid making it uncomfortable for her.

"Wow, this menu is exotic." Alistair read through the list of courses that they'd be served aloud. "Foie gras, escargots de Bourgogne, tete de veau. I can't even pronounce these, let alone eat them."

But Amelia was too distracted by something else, and Alistair noticed. "What's wrong?" he asked. "Looks like something's bothering you."

"I still can't get over why Aunt Evelyne booked the lover's special for us. I mean, it's only our first date, and she's already acting like we're married."

He shrugged. "I'm sure she means no harm. She just wanted us to have a nice night out, that's all. But if you don't like it, we can always go somewhere else. Burgers, maybe?"

"No, it's fine. We can stay. I just don't want to feel like we're moving too fast."

"Hey, Amelia." He turned his body slightly and held onto her hands. The tingling sensation shivered up her body once more. "We can move as slow as you like. This... experience, or whatever you wanna call it—"

"Fucked-up situation?"

"That." He smiled at her again, a look of comfort and compassion shining through his eyes as he did so. "This fucked-up situation is all new to me, too. I'm just as nervous as you are."

"So, why'd you agree to her idea, anyway?"

He sighed. Then he paused and took a deep breath. "Amber."

"Amber?"

"Yeah, Amber. She was my girlfriend. My girlfriend of

seven years, to be exact. Until... until she got killed by a drunk driver one night." He took another deep breath.

"I'm so sorry."

"Don't be. It was my fault, anyway."

"How?"

"Well, Amber was drinking at a party with some of her friends and called me to come get her, but I couldn't because I was stuck at work. Long story short, she decided to get into her car anyway and, apparently, when two drunk drivers collide, it only ends in a fatality. I told her to just stay at her friend's, but she started throwing a fit and insisted that if I didn't come get her, she'd just drive herself."

"I'm sorry," Amelia said again, feeling awkward in the moment. "Are you okay?"

Alistair sniffled. "Yeah, I'm okay. And I'm sorry for unloading all this on you. Your aunt heard about my story from my mother and was only trying to pull me out of my slump and get me back out there. Mentioned that she has a niece also going through a rough time, and that we could either be happy together or sit in that slump together. Her words, not mine."

Amelia chuckled. "Definitely sounds like her."

"So, what about your situation? What's your story?"

But she just shook her head. "I don't really want to talk about it."

"I understand." He scooted himself closer to her. "If you ever do, I'm here." And then he wrapped his arm around Amelia's shoulders.

She didn't fight it, and instead, leaned her head down against him. In that moment, it just felt right, and though she didn't want to admit it, Amelia felt herself drawn closer and closer to the stranger beside her.

Chapter Four

"Amelia, honey! Don't forget. Alistair will be here in twenty minutes to pick you up!" her mother shouted up from the base of the stairs.

Amelia rolled over in her bed, the sheets tangling in between her legs as she dragged them with her. She could feel her head pounding from the lack of sleep. Despite being miles and miles away from her dorm, she still found it difficult to force herself to put down the phone.

Lucas Liard still hadn't responded to her, not even a hint that he'd reached out. And even though she quite enjoyed her first date with Alistair, she found herself continuing to scroll through guy after guy, trying to find that *perfect* person.

It also didn't help that Melody talked her ear off last night, asking about Alistair and everything about him, from his looks to his personality, even his estimated weight.

She finally managed to roll herself off the bed and grab her phone, checking the time. Noon.

"Ugh, did I really just blow my entire morning in bed?" Amelia asked herself and grabbed a towel off from the floor. Today was her second date with Alistair, and after smelling his delicious cologne from the night before, she couldn't repay him with her stench of onions and mildew.

Amelia still didn't know how she felt about him. Alistair. Sure, he was definitely the looker, a man whom everyone would stop whatever they were doing for and gawk at his beautiful eyes and charming smile. But she still couldn't imagine herself being with him. She wanted Lucas, who was a ten. David was a solid nine, and Alistair, half past nine at best. He definitely didn't reach up to Lucas' caliber, and Amelia questioned whether she was making the right decision.

"It's three dates," she reminded herself. "Just three dates. If by the end of date three, I find that I still don't like him, I'll never have to see him again. Easy."

Ten minutes later, she hopped out of the shower and into her closet. Today was beach day, an activity that Amelia felt even more nervous about than the lover's special. She'd always been body conscious, and wearing a bikini or anything revealing was one of the worst feelings in the world for her. She didn't even know if she owned a swimsuit as she always preferred mountains over beaches.

But she couldn't blame Alistair. It wasn't like he had a say either in what their dates were going to be. Hell, he probably hated the ideas as much as she did, but he's just too polite to say anything.

Amelia spent the next few minutes rummaging through her closet again, but came up short on finding a swimsuit. She eventually settled for a mini skirt with a tank top, the closest thing she could find. She then walked back over to her vanity and ran a brush through her thick hair when she heard the doorbell ring.

"Amelia!" her mother called again.

"I'm coming!" She looked down at her brush, clumps of hair knotted everywhere. But that wasn't what she was focused on. She was focused on the engraving. *A&D*. Amelia and

David. David had gotten that brush for her on their first-year anniversary. He told her how she had the most beautiful hair he'd ever seen and wanted her to take care of it. And even though she'd thrown away most of the gifts that David had ever gotten for her, she couldn't find it in herself to throw away this brush. It had become her favorite over the years, and part of her still wanted to hold onto that memory of her first serious boyfriend.

ALISTAIR WAS GLOWING beneath the sun rays when Amelia made her way downstairs. He had a towel slung over his left arm, his hair slicked back, and his tanned abs glistening as he leaned against the doorway. He had on swimming trunks and carried a picnic basket, leaving little to the imagination.

"Is that what you're wearing to the beach?" he asked Amelia while raising a brow when he saw her walk down the stairs. A slight curve formed on his lips, and it looked like he was trying to hold in a laugh.

"Hey, don't judge. It's all I have. I don't go to the beach very often."

"I can tell, but you still look great."

"Aw, look at you two teasing each other! So sweet!" Amelia's mother interrupted them with a tray of warm chocolate chip cookies in her hands. "I remember when your father and I used to tease each other. Of course, now he barely remembers my name. Here, take a few of these cookies before you go. I just baked them." She held the tray out in between them, nudging at them both and refusing to leave until they each grabbed one.

"Thank you, Mrs. Ainsworth," Alistair mumbled, holding the cookie up. "These smell delicious."

"Yeah, Mom, delicious. We should really get going."

Amelia jumped in as an attempt to save them both from bagging a pouch of cookies and bringing it with them.

The Jersey shore wasn't far from where Amelia's parents lived. It didn't have the best beaches, or the cleanest, and the weather wasn't the warmest on a windy March afternoon, but it was another one of Aunt Evelyne's wishes, and they didn't want to disappoint. Besides, Alistair was starting to grow hotter and hotter in Amelia's eyes every time she saw him. And those abs, those sexy abs that she just wanted to run her fingers over... they were enough to make her second guess her choice in men.

When Alistair pulled up into the parking lot of Cape May, they realized that theirs was the only car there.

"There's nobody here," Amelia mumbled.

"I kinda figured. It's pretty chilly out today. Why your aunt decided to choose the coldest day of the week for an activity meant for the heat is beyond me." He turned to Amelia. "We can go if you like. Somewhere indoors and warm."

But Amelia shook her head. "No, let's stay. I've never been to the beach when there's nobody else here. This might actually be fun."

"I agree! No drunk dads chasing after their screaming kids. No beach ball bouncing off my head when I'm trying to enjoy the sun."

"Man, sounds like a rough experience. I never thought I'd meet someone who hates the beach more than I do." Amelia smiled and took a bite of her cookie.

Alistair smiled back and wiped away a crumb from the corner of her mouth. "I don't hate it per se, more like I hate people ruining the experience for me."

"I know the feeling."

"But, hey, enough talk about how much we both hate people. We have the entire beach to ourselves. Let's go out there and enjoy it!" Alistair reached into the back and grabbed the towel and basket. Then he skipped over to Amelia's side and opened the passenger door for her. "Shall we?" he asked, extending a hand out to her.

"We shall," she responded and grabbed it, allowing him to lift her off her seat, her skirt bunched up behind her.

He continued to hold her hand as he led her out to the vast open shore before them. The waves swayed gently across the water, colliding with the sand before stealing some away as they retreated to where they started. Alistair unfolded the towel just a few feet from the frigid water, and they both sat down and leaned back, their elbows digging into the sand and creating craters beneath them.

"Tell me, Amelia. Why don't you like going to the beach?" Alistair asked after staring out into the ocean for quite some time.

"When did I say I don't like it?"

"You didn't. But you did mention how you don't go often, and your lack of a swimsuit makes me think that you prefer going somewhere else during your free time."

"It's true. I'm more of a mountain girl. There's just something about standing up at the tallest peak you can find and looking down at the vast wonders below you that can't be replaced by water and sand, you know?"

"I totally get what you mean. I myself enjoy mountains much more than beaches also. But I think the journey is what I'm more drawn to than the destination. It just feels very rewarding knowing that despite the struggle, the hard work I put into something will eventually pay off." Alistair agreed.

"So, would you say competition is more your style than remaining laidback and passive?" Amelia asked, causing Alistair to form a perplexed look on his face.

"Uhm, I guess. I tend to see myself as a go-getter."

"Well...," Amelia quickly stood up and tapped Alistair on

the shoulder, "you're it! Catch me before I reach the lifeguard post, and you win." She bolted off, her laughter trailing behind.

"Oh, you're on," Alistair shouted back and quickly stood up, running after her.

Amelia was a track star in high school, and was pretty fast for a girl. She saw herself as a competitive person as well, and she was certain that she'd win the race. However, less than ten feet from the finish line, Amelia found herself being hoisted into the air. Alistair had caught up to her and grabbed her by the waist, swinging her in the air, the two of them laughing.

"Gotcha!" He chuckled. Then he swung Amelia around one more time before laying her down against the stand, hovering over her as he said, "Told you I'm competitive. I also had an unfair advantage. I was a track star in high school."

"So was I!" Amelia yelled back. "I just don't have ten pounds of muscle in each leg to propel me forward." She playfully hit Alistair on the chest, her fingers trailing down his abs as she brought her hand back into herself.

The two fell silent for a moment as they both gazed into each other's eyes.

"Are you feeling what I'm feeling?" Alistair finally asked.

"Cold?" Amelia responded.

"Exactly. We should get back to the car. We can eat our lunch in there."

Amelia nodded, and as she stood up, Alistair wrapped his strong arms around her. She could feel his hard abs pressed against the side of her body, and she felt her heart skipping faster and faster as he breathed down her neck. He'd pulled her so close to him that any closer, they'd become one person. And when Alistair thought she wouldn't notice, he leaned down and kissed the top of her head, causing a smile to form on Amelia's face.

When they eventually got back to the car, Alistair cranked

the heat up and pulled his jacket out from the trunk for her to wrap around herself. It smelled of old spice and vanilla, just like he'd smelled on their first date. She pulled it tighter around herself, crossing one leg over the other for extra warmth.

He noticed and reached his hand back to pull the towel up front. "Here, use this to warm up your legs."

"What about you? Aren't you cold?"

Alistair shrugged. "Don't worry about me. I can stand it. You need it more than I do."

"Thank you." She took a bite of the turkey and Swiss cheese sandwich that Aunt Evelyne had prepared for them, and then swallowed hard. "Hey, Alistair?"

"Yeah?" he asked after taking a bite from his own sandwich.

"I think I'm ready to talk about my past relationship now."

At that, he lowered his sandwich back down, shifted his body closer to her, and gave her his full attention. "I'm all ears. Treat me like I'm a therapist."

She giggled. "Should I lie back also?"

"If you want."

"His name's David. We met when I was finishing up high school, and he was my first serious boyfriend. He meant everything to me. But of course, I was naïve and stupid enough to believe that high school sweethearts really were that common. He didn't always treat me the best, using me and treating me like I was his slave, but I let it go. I thought that's how relationships are supposed to be." She paused for a minute, and Alistair reached a hand out to tuck a strand of hair behind Amelia's right ear. "But I was foolish," she then continued, "to believe that he actually loved me the way I loved him. Two months before we finally broke up, I found a pair of panties in the back seat of his car."

Alistair continued listening without saying a word while he reached over to hold her hands in his.

"Can you believe it? I caught him cheating on me, and I still stayed, telling myself that it's just a mistake, and that he still loves me. He didn't even deny it!" She sighed. "Anyway, two months after that, he found out that he'd knocked her up, got her pregnant, and just dumped me without saying another word. Since then, I've stopped going out on dates until I know I've found the perfect one. I can't risk getting hurt again."

"Do you think it's a mistake that you're here with me now? Do you think I'll hurt you like David had?" Alistair squeezed tighter.

"Honestly," Amelia admitted, "I thought so at first. I thought my aunt was tired of me being single, so she forced me to go out with you. Now? Now I'm not so sure."

"What do you mean?"

"I like being around you, Alistair. These past two days have been amazing. I'm... I'm just not sure if you're the perfect guy yet. Please don't be mad."

And he wasn't. "It's okay, Amelia. After going through such heartbreak like you have, I completely understand why you have your standards. And I know that reaching those standards is a hard role to play. There's a chance that we're not perfect for each other. But there's also a chance that we are. You never know until you've tested out the waters."

"Thanks for understanding, Alistair. And I don't mean to offend you."

"Not offended at all." Suddenly, he leaned over closer to her, caressing her face with his hand, and planting a soft kiss on her lips. She kissed back at first, for a minute or two, before pulling away.

"I... I can't," she whispered, causing Alistair to retreat to his side of the car.

"Sorry, I'm sorry. I should've asked."

"No, no, don't be sorry. I… I just don't know how I feel about you yet." Amelia explained. "I liked the kiss. I really did. I just don't want to get my heart broken again."

Alistair remained silent, his heart obviously stunned.

"I think maybe you should take me home," she muttered with a heavy heart.

AMELIA COULDN'T SHAKE the feeling of guilt away later that night. She felt awful about the way she treated Alistair. He'd been so nice to her, and she couldn't even give him a simple kiss in return. She tossed and turned in her bed, frustrated that she couldn't shake away the feeling. Eventually, she gave up and sat up in bed. She reached over to grab her phone and dialed.

"Hello?"

"Hey, Alistair."

"Amelia? What's wrong? Is everything okay?"

"Yeah, I'm sorry for calling so late. I felt really bad about earlier, for pushing you away, and I wanted to apologize. I hope you're not mad at me."

"I'm not. Don't worry about it. It was a shock at first. I thought we were getting along, connecting. It just took me by surprise when you pushed me away."

"I know. I'm really sorry. I hope this doesn't ruin our date tomorrow."

"Nah, I'm over it. Pick you up at five tomorrow?"

"I'll be waiting."

Chapter Five

The next day, Amelia had a few hours to spare before her third and final date with Alistair. She still hadn't decided whether she wanted to continue seeing him after, or if she'd just return to her old ways on her trusty app, but that was a decision for later that night.

She scheduled an appointment at the salon to get her hair done, not to impress him, but because her hair was matted from not being groomed in over three years.

But on her way there, she saw the backside of a familiar figure, someone she knew, someone—

"David?"

The man spun around, and it was none other than her ex. "Amelia!" he greeted. "It's been awhile." He walked over to give her a hug, but her body only tensed. "What are you doing here? Aren't you still in school?"

"It's spring break. I came home to visit my family. Where's what's-her-name?"

"Rebecca? Oh, we broke it off. Funny story! Turned out the kid isn't even mine. She'd been shacking it up with guys all around town."

"You deserve it," Amelia mumbled.

"Sorry, what was that?"

"You kinda had it coming, David. Karma has its way of nipping you in the ass when you decide to screw over someone you'd promised to love forever."

David's face dropped, his usually happy-go-lucky style turning into someone who looked like they'd just been beaten twice and pushed off a cliff.

"I-I'm sorry," Amelia apologized. "I didn't mean to come off that harsh. I'm still a little bitter, you know?"

"No, you're right. I do deserve it. You shouldn't have been treated the way I treated you, and I'm truly sorry for everything I've done to you." Then he stepped closer to Amelia and held her by the hands. "Truth is, I've never stopped thinking about you, ever since we broke up—"

"You mean, ever since you dumped me," she jumped in.

"Right, I'm sorry for breaking up with you. But truth is, Amelia, I've never been able to replace you. Rebecca, she didn't mean anything to me, just a fling, something to entertain myself with, but you? Amelia, you're my everything, my high school sweetheart, and a huge part of me still believes that we're meant to be together, until the very end, just like we'd always promised each other."

"Yeah, until you cheated on me," Amelia mumbled and backed away slightly.

"Do you still love me?"

"What?" That got her attention.

"Do you still love me?" David repeated.

Amelia felt her stomach drop. Did she? To be honest, she'd spent so much time swiping from guy to guy that she never really stopped to think about David. But now that he was here, standing in front of her and professing how he felt about her, she felt all her past feelings, all the feelings she'd tried so hard to erase, all rushing back. She'd been with David for so long, her first love, and the person she created the most memories with. And she even swore to herself and Melody that she was over him, that she'd never run back to someone who could so easily run away from her.

So... so why was she finding herself being drawn back to him? Why was she suddenly remembering the happy times they've shared together?

"I... I...," Amelia stuttered.

"Say it, say it, Amelia. Do you still love me?" He held on tighter to her hands and inched in even closer. She could smell the scent of his aftershave, a scent that made her want to gag, nothing like the delicious vanilla fragrance of Alistair.

"I... I... don't," Amelia finally said and pulled her hands away. "I... I have to go."

So close. She was so close to walking straight back into her past, back into the arms of someone who left her for the wolves while he claimed another queen. And it took smelling him to help her remember that she didn't need him in her life anymore, that she was happier without him. She quickly jogged home, skipping that hair appointment she'd booked.

She had to get ready for her date with Alistair.

"Amelia! Alistair's here!" Amelia heard her mother shout for the third time that night.

"I said, I'm coming!" she shouted back.

Amelia walked over to her vanity to observe her outfit for the night. She didn't know what the occasion was. The only hint she'd gotten was to "dress for a fun occasion," whatever that meant. But whatever it was, blue skinny jeans with a black leather jacket over a white T-shirt, and her hair tied up in a high ponytail, were going to have to do the trick.

"Amelia!" She heard the piercing scream of her mother once again.

"Ugh!" Amelia grabbed her purse and started to walk out the door. But then she stopped. "Forgot my gloss." And she reached into her vanity drawer to pull it out. She froze when she saw the brush. *A&D*. Still written on it as clear as day. Amelia picked it up, ran a finger across the engraving, and then threw it into her trash can before walking out the door and heading downstairs.

"Hey, beautiful," Alistair said with a smile. Amelia blushed. She hadn't heard anyone call her that in a long time, and the beautiful bouquet of roses in his hands definitely made those words sound much, much sweeter. "These are for you," he continued as if he'd read her mind, and extended his hands out to give her the roses.

"Thank you, Alistair." Amelia extended her own arms out and grabbed the roses. "I'll go put these in water straight away."

"Nope! Let me. I got it," her mother interrupted and grabbed them away. "I'll just bring these into the kitchen. You two stay here and talk."

As she skipped away, Alistair closed the gap between himself and Amelia. He reached a hand out again and tucked a strand of hair behind her ear. "Now that your mother is gone, are you going to tell me what's wrong?"

"What do you mean?"

"Amelia, I could see it on your face as soon as you walked down those stairs. Something's bothering you."

"What? No, nothing's bothering me. I'm fine!" Amelia tried her best to maintain her poker face. It wasn't like he was wrong; Alistair was definitely right. But she couldn't tell him about running into David. And how all her feelings for him shot back into her mind. It wasn't a conversation she was ready to have with someone yet, especially not with someone she'd probably stop seeing after tonight.

She looked up at Alistair while she was lost in thought, expecting to see an angry look plastered across his face, but instead, he grinned at her.

"W-Why are you smiling?" she asked.

"Heh, you're cute when you're flustered."

"I'm not flustered!"

"Hey, it's okay. You don't have to tell me anything. I was just trying to help. But like I said before, if you ever want to talk to me about anything, I'll be here. But I won't pressure you."

"So," Amelia crossed her arms in front of her chest, "where're we headed tonight?"

"Hmm, it's a surprise." Alistair continued to grin.

"Well, if I know Aunt Evelyne, I bet it's something boring and traditional like the movies or something," Amelia guessed.

"True, it would be something like that... if she had chosen for us."

"What do you mean?"

Alistair grabbed Amelia's right hand and squeezed. "Tonight's destination... is all my idea. And I want it to be a surprise."

"Well, I can't wait to see it," Amelia replied, clenching together the fingers on her other hand. She hated surprises, but she couldn't tell him that.

"Shall we get going?"

"We shall."

And as the two walked out the door, Amelia's mother followed them. "Wait! Before you go, you two have to try one of my brownies. Freshly baked, straight from the oven!"

"Mom, stop trying to make us fat." Amelia crossed her arms over her chest in protest.

"It's okay, I don't mind," Alistair responded. "I'll take one." And as he did, Amelia ushered him out the door.

"Sorry about my mother. She's not from here originally. It's traditional for her to want to fatten people up."

"Ha, yeah, I was just going to ask. Does she do this with all her guests?"

"Unfortunately, yes. So, are you ready to tell me the surprise? Where are we headed?"

"Hmm, not quite yet." When they reached his car, Alistair pulled out a blindfold. "Here, put this on."

"Why? Trying to kidnap me? I'm already willingly going out with you."

"Ah, but how else will I be sure that you'll stay with me forever?" It clearly sounded like a joke, but Amelia still got offended.

"Excuse me? What makes you think I'm yours?"

"I-I-I didn't. It was just a joke," Alistair quickly apologized. "You know, how I know you're not mine, and kidnapping you is the only way I can make you mine?" He began crazily gesturing his hands, his face growing flustered.

"Make me yours? Who do you think I am?" Amelia's face turned red. She knew she was unnecessarily taking her anger out on Alistair. Seeing David today just brought back all the bad memories of her past.

"I'm really sorry, Amelia. Truly. I didn't mean to offend you or hurt you. I just thought it was a funny joke, you know, with the blindfold." Then he shoved it back into his pocket. "But if that bothers you, you don't have to put it on. We can just go, if you'd like. Or we can cut this date short, and you can go back home. Whatever you want. I just want to make you happy."

Amelia's facial muscles loosened their tension, and her eyes of anger turned into eyes of sadness. "No, we can go. It's my fault. I get that you were only trying to make a joke, and I definitely overreacted. I'm sorry. Can you forgive me?"

Alistair was quick to smile and embrace her into a hug. "Of course! We all make mistakes, say things we shouldn't. I get it. It's no big deal!" Then he released the hug and jutted out his elbow. "Shall we?"

"We shall." Amelia looped her arm through the gap created, and he led her into the passenger side of his car. "And yes, I'll wear the blindfold."

AND IT WAS DEFINITELY to Amelia's shock when she took the blindfold off thirty minutes later, something she'd never expected to see. Alistair had pulled into the parking lot of an arcade! And Amelia hated arcades more than she hated anything else. The bright lights, the loud music, sticky kids running around, the smell of vomit and piss. And top it all off with rigged and expensive crappy games that serve no purpose other than to rob you of your entire bank account and give you a shitty teddy bear, worth no more than five bucks, in return.

"So, what do you think?" Alistair turned his head as he shut off the engine and looked at her.

Ugh, I can't tell him I hate it; that'll crush him. "I-I love it," she said instead, secretly screaming to herself on the inside.

Amelia used to love arcades as a kid, carnivals, specifically. Her parents would bring her and her brother to one once a year, and the rushed feeling of soaring high above the ground on a rollercoaster or stuffing her face with cotton candy, while her brother challenged their dad in the arcade, was one of the best she'd ever experienced.

But that all changed when she turned eleven. Their family vacation to Wildwood. The trip where she found out that she'd been forgotten. She remembered complaining of stomach pains after stuffing her face with funnel cake and ice cream, and when she came back out from using the restroom, her mother was gone. She'd promised that she was going to wait for her, that she was going to stay right outside until Amelia came back out.

And when Amelia failed to find her mother after looking around, she began to panic. She ran up and down the board-walk, screaming for her mother, her father, her brother, anybody she recognized who could help her. But with no luck. When she decided to try the arcade, hoping that her father and brother were still battling it out, she found the place much scarier than she'd remembered. The bright lights, the loud sounds, the screaming kids and adults. They were all just too much handle for a young child who was already stressed out about being left alone.

Abandoned.

"Mom?" She remembered crying out loud, only to be pushed to the ground by a horde.

It took several hours later and a long wait at the security office for Amelia to eventually find out that Jason had injured himself while playing Dance Dance Revolution, and both her parents were in such a rush to take him to the hospital that they'd completely forgotten about her.

"It was just an accident," they'd say. But deep down, Amelia knew they wouldn't have done the same if she were the one to have gotten injured.

"Great! Ready to head inside? I can't wait to show you my favorite games." Alistair clapped his hands together in excitement, and once again, rushed to the other side to open the passenger door for her.

But when Amelia walked in, all the memories of her past came rushing back. The lights. The screaming children. The distinct stench of putrid vomit mixed with overly buttery popcorn. She held her breath, trying her best to not hurl when Alistair pulled her toward the basketball hoops.

"Challenge you in a game?" he asked, picking up a ball and handing it over to her.

Amelia shook her head and pushed it away. "No, thanks. It's not really my thing. But you go ahead. I'll watch."

Alistair scrunched his forehead and rubbed his chin dramatically with his fingers. "Are you sure? We can always go and play something else! Anything you want!"

"I'm sure." Amelia nodded her head. "I'm more of a watcher, anyway." *More of a watcher? Did I really just say that? What a stupid thing to say!*

"Alright, if you insist. Watch me make this awesome trick shot!"

Amelia watched with boredom as Alistair spun around in a circle before shooting the ball, touching nothing but net as the ball smoothly slid into the hoop.

"Yes!" he shouted.

The rest of the night continued similarly as Alistair played every game possible inside the arcade, a true kid in a candy store, as Amelia just stood by his side, yawning and playing on her phone. She made sure Alistair wasn't looking as she discretely scrolled through Lucas' social media profile, admiring the tanned abs and glistening smile in his most recent pictures.

"Hey, Amelia!" A voice distracted her, and when she looked up, Alistair was holding a pink stuffed teddy bear. "I got this for you. Took all my tickets, but I really wanted to get you something."

She grabbed it and muttered, "Thanks."

"What's wrong? Do you not like it?"

"It's okay, I guess. It's just that I could've bought this at Walmart for half the cost of what it took to play all these games."

Alistair's face fell. "Well... I thought it was a nice gesture. We had fun, and I only played all those games so I could win enough tickets to get something for you."

But Amelia shook her head. "No, Alistair. *You* had fun. *You* spent all this money getting a cheap toy. All I did was watch you."

"B-But you said that's what you wanted. I'm sorry, Amelia. I didn't realize you weren't having any fun. I asked you several times if you wanted to play, but you kept saying no."

"Because I hate arcades! I'm sorry, Alistair. Here, take your bear back. I'm going home. Thanks for the date, but I don't think there will be another one."

His face fell even harder, low enough to make Amelia feel sorry for him if she wasn't already in such a frustrated mood. "I understand. Can I at least take you home?"

"No, I'll just call my mom." Amelia quickly threw back and walked out the glass doors.

Chapter Six

Aweek later, back at her dorm, Amelia found herself calling her ex, David.

"Hello?"

"Hey, David. It's me, Amelia."

"Oh, what do you want?"

"I was just thinking. Remember how when we ran into each other the other day, you said that part of you still believes that we're meant to be together?"

"Yeah...?"

"Well, I was wondering... do you want to give us another shot? See if this whole high school sweetheart thing will really pay off? Maybe we were too young to commit when we dated before, but we've both grown now. It might actually work out."

"Uhm, no. I don't think so."

"Why not? You said we could work."

"Yeah, Amelia. I did. But when I asked you if you still loved me, you flat out said no and ran away. That fucking hurt. I stood there, out in the open, vulnerable, and you just rejected me. No way in hell am I falling for your mind tricks again."

"But David, that wasn't—"

"Goodbye, Amelia."

And just like that, David hung up. And when she tried calling again, she found out that he'd blocked her. Her heart felt broken, crushed, just like it had felt when he left her the first time. After such a horrible date with Alistair last week, she was sure that David was the one for her, and that no one else could ever compare. Unfortunately for her, he didn't have the same thought, and Amelia was left all alone again.

She even tried to take her mind off the pain by resuming her daily ritual of scrolling through eligible bachelors, but even those didn't seem as interesting to her anymore. She didn't know what she was feeling, but her mind felt distracted by something. By someone.

"Ah, Ms. Ainsworth, I see that, once again, you're using my class as your own personal naptime." Amelia flung her head up and found Professor Ambone and the rest of her class staring at her, as if her life were on a never-ending loop, and spring break had never happened.

"Huh? I-I'm sorry. I-I'm sorry. It won't happen again," Amelia stuttered.

"Well, I sure hope not, especially if you pass this final exam and move on from my class."

"What? Exam?" Amelia turned to Melody as Professor Ambone proceeded to hand out the small blue notebooks.

"Aw, Amelia, don't tell me you forgot! Did you really stay up all night again swiping instead of studying?"

"What? No, I just couldn't sleep, that's all. My mind's been distracted lately."

"Lucas again?"

"Ahem!" Professor Ambone suddenly appeared in front of them. "Ladies, time to put the chit-chat away."

Amelia gulped as he placed the small blue notebook in front of her, followed by a thick stack of papers she assumed were the problems. She took one look at the first one, and her eyes opened wide in horror. She looked over at Melody, who was quickly scribbling away, and then she looked at Professor Ambone, who was staring straight at her from the front, as if he were expecting her to do something she shouldn't. She quickly looked down at the first problem again, groaning, flipping through to the other pages to see if she knew any of the other ones, and started scribbling away.

After class, she met up with Melody in the cafeteria, throwing a slice of pizza onto her tray just to have it, but Amelia found that she didn't have an appetite. When she sat down, Melody was already at their favorite spot, digging into her salad.

"You left class pretty quickly today," Melody said. "I'm guessing the exam was a breeze for you?"

"Are you kidding me?! I didn't know a single answer. I only handed my stuff in so I could get the hell out of there. I could only sit there and stare for so long. I'm pretty sure I failed."

"Lia! Why didn't you study? I reminded you every day for the past week to make sure you're prepared. What the hell were you doing instead?"

"I don't even know." Amelia slid into her seat. "It's like, ever since I came back from spring break, my mind has been elsewhere."

She nodded. "Is it because of Alistair?"

"Alistair?"

"Yeah, whatever happened to him? He seemed like such a perfect match for you," Melody asked, taking a bite of her salad.

Amelia shrugged. "Just didn't really connect like I'd hoped. Besides, I only went out with him to make Aunt

Evelyne happy. Three dates. That's what I promised. Nothing more. He's not really my type."

"You know, Amelia, for someone who says she wants a boyfriend, you sure are awfully picky. I thought Alistair was a great guy. Incredibly sexy, too."

"Yeah, but he's not... he's not Lucas Liard."

Then suddenly, her phone rang. Amelia pulled it out of her jacket pocket and saw a message from none other than Lucas Liard himself.

LUCAS

Hey, Amelia. Saw you super liked me. Down to grab a drink tonight?

"Oh my god, oh my god!" Amelia practically danced in her seat. "You'll never guess who just asked me out! Lucas! Do you know how long I've been waiting for this moment? How much I've been obsessing over him?"

"Oh, I sure do. But don't you think it's a bit odd how he blew you off for so long, and he's just *now* getting back to you? If he really liked you, he wouldn't have waited."

"Nah, I'm sure he just had other things going on. I mean, it's Lucas Liard, the most eligible bachelor in town, maybe in the entire county! And he wants to go out with *me*. Me! I can't pass up the chance."

"Hmm, I don't know, Amelia. I don't trust him. What if he's just using you?"

"Mel, look, I don't have time for your rational judgment right now. I gotta go. I need as much time as I can get to prepare for tonight. I'll call you later!" Amelia rushed through her sentence and grabbed her bag, leaving her pizza to grow cold on the cafeteria table and rushing out the door.

"Do I look stunning, or do I look stunning?" Amelia asked herself as she danced in front of the floor-length mirror in her dorm later that night. "Fit to be Lucas Liard's queen, I might add?"

The time was seven, and Lucas said he'd be here to pick her up for their date. Amelia had been preparing for the past three hours, making sure her makeup was perfect, every strand of hair on her head was perfect, her face free from blemishes or wrinkles. She was finally going out on a date with the man she couldn't stop stalking, and she wanted to make a good first impression, give him something that he's never going to forget. Make him remember her forever.

"Perfect," Amelia slipped in her last earring and tucked a strand of loose hair behind her ear, "and just in time."

She picked up her phone, expecting a text from Lucas telling her that he was outside. But she saw nothing. Ten minutes soon passed, then fifteen, then thirty. Still nothing.

"I guess he's not coming." Amelia sighed and took off her shoes. "Something probably came up. I'll text him tomorrow and see if he wants to reschedule."

And then something. Her phone dinged, and it was a message from Lucas.

LUCAS

Hey, sorry, my car broke down, and I couldn't come get you. Do you think you can meet me at Duggard's Bar? I live right near there.

Duggard's Bar was nearly forty minutes away from where Amelia lived, and she'd let Melody borrow her car tonight since she'd expected Lucas to pick her up. She could always hail a cab, an Uber, something cozy to take her downtown, but being so late at night, it'd be a struggle just to find one that wouldn't charge her an arm and leg.

But she couldn't say no, as inconveniencing as it was for her. If she canceled on him, she may never get another chance to go out with him, killing any hope she had of being with him.

"The bus it is, I guess." Amelia quickly messaged Lucas back, telling him that she'd be there in about an hour. Fortunately for her, he quickly messaged her back, saying that he'd still be there waiting for her.

With a smile, Amelia threw her shoes back on and grabbed the little cash she had from her desk drawer. "Three dollars in singles. Should be enough to cover the fare."

A little over an hour and a dreadful bus ride later, Amelia finally made it to Duggard's Bar. It was packed when she walked in, something she was never a fan of. She tended to stay away from scenes where she struggled just to hear herself talk. But she didn't come this far just to back out now. And so, she squeezed her way through the drunken crowd to find Lucas.

When she eventually did, he was sitting at the bar, talking to a woman.

"Hey, Lucas, who's this?" Amelia asked as she approached them, gesturing to the bartender for a glass of water.

"Amelia, babe! You made it! You had me worried sick that something had happened to you," Lucas practically screamed when he saw her, the smell of alcohol pungent on his breath. "Oh, this? This is Lucy. She was just keeping me company while I waited for you." He turned to grin at Lucy, who slapped him hard across the cheek and stormed away.

"That's... weird," Amelia said. "Is she mad about something?"

"Nah." Lucas waved a hand. "Probably just on her period or something. Hey, let me buy you a drink. What's your style? Long Island? Cranny vodka?"

"Just a beer is fine."

"Simple, I like that." He gestured to the bartender. "One beer, my good man."

"Lucas, I have to ask, why'd it take you so long to message me back? I know you saw my message."

"Message? No, no, you see, my phone is a little messed up sometimes. It sends read receipts even if I hadn't actually read them. Such an odd glitch. I should really have someone take a look at it. I just saw your message last night. Figured you're cute. So, here we are!"

"That... that *is* a strange glitch." Amelia struggled to believe him, but she didn't want to risk saying anything that'd cause him to leave.

"Hey, it's a bit loud in here, don't you think? What do you say we go somewhere much quieter?"

Best idea I've heard all night. "Count me in! Where were you thinking?"

"Back to my place? My apartment's just down the road; we could walk there."

Amelia nodded and followed Lucas out of the bar and out the back door. He was walking so fast, his body swaying from side to side as he struggled to keep his drunken self upright. Amelia struggled to keep up with him, her heels stabbing into the soles of her feet as she ran.

Fifteen minutes later, Amelia stopped running when Lucas stood in front of a run-down ten-story apartment building, waving for her to hurry up. He unlocked the front door and led her up to the third floor.

"Here we are! Welcome to my bachelor pad!" he announced as they both walked in.

The first thing that Amelia noticed was the smell, the smell of musty day-old pizza and aftershave. The second thing she noticed was how much of a slob Lucas was. There were clothes strewn all over his raggedy sofa and computer, beer bottles forming a rug over the stained carpet, and pizza boxes were scattered in every corner that Amelia could find.

"Nice... nice place you have here," Amelia mumbled, pushing aside a pile of clothes to find a spot for herself to sit on the sofa. *Geez, and I thought I was messy.*

"Sorry about all the mess. I wasn't expecting to have company tonight," Lucas apologized and sat beside her. The stench of alcohol was way more prominent now that they were out of the bar.

"It's fine."

"So, Amelia," he leaned back and threw his arm over his shoulders, "tell me, what is it that you really want?"

"What do you mean?"

"I mean, why'd you wanna go out with me? Meet me at a bar?"

Amelia felt confused. She'd never been asked that question before. A date is just a date, something people do when they like each other. *Why's he interrogating me?*

"Uhm, I think you're cute, and I wanted to get to know you better."

Lucas pretended to think for a bit before shaking his head in reply. "Nah, I think you want something more than that." He leaned in closer. "I think you wanna fuck me. And you know what? I wanna fuck you, too."

Then he pounced on her, pressing his lips against hers, and began peeling off her clothes.

"Lucas, stop. You're drunk. We shouldn't do this!" Amelia struggled to speak through Lucas' slobbering lips, his roaming hands groping all parts of her body.

"I'm not drunk, just horny. Come on, I know you want this. So hot." He moved his lips down to her neck, then to her breasts, before Amelia pushed him off her and onto the ground.

"I said, no!" she screamed and pulled her clothes back around her body.

"What the hell, bitch?" Lucas screamed back from the floor. "Why the *fuck* did you wanna go out with me if you didn't want this?"

"I-I-I just wanted to get to know you."

"Bullshit! If you're not gonna put out, I want you out!"

"But Lucas—"

"I said, out!"

Amelia picked her bag off from the sofa and ran toward the door, kicking aside a couple beer bottles in the process. Tears were streaming down her face, ruining the perfectly contoured makeup that she'd spent hours putting on. Lucas turned out to be nothing like the embodiment of perfection that Amelia had longed for. He wasn't her perfect match, not even a sad attempt at a match. How could she have been such a fool, thinking that someone like Lucas, a fuck boy, would ever want anything more from her than sex?

Walking out into the cold, Amelia stood there waiting for the bus. According to the schedule online, there was still one left that ran at this hour. Tears continued to stream down her face as she thought back to how Alistair always made sure that she was warm and comfortable in his car, always her knight in shining armor and ready to pick her up.

Alistair had always been there for her, the complete opposite of David and Lucas. He understood when she overreacted, forgiving her in an instant. He was the perfect gentleman when she told him that she wanted space, and he never walked ahead of her, always remaining by her side and holding her hand, making sure that she was happy and safe.

"Alistair," Amelia said to herself. "How could I have been so wrong about you? How could I have treated you the way I did?"

Chapter Seven

That weekend, Amelia found herself driving back home once again. She'd failed her physics exam, meaning she'd have to retake Ambone's class over the summer, but that was the least of her worries.

Her Aunt Evelyne had died; she found out the morning after her disastrous date with Lucas. The Leukemia had spread to her lungs, and she died from suffocation and lack of oxygen in her sleep. Her aunt was like a second mother to Amelia, taking care of her, cooking her favorite meals, playing with her when her mother was at work. She should've been sadder, more devastated, but the events of her own shitty love life had numbed her to everything else around her.

When she arrived home, cars were piled up outside her parents' house. The door was cracked open, and Amelia made her way inside after she'd pulled into the driveway. The entire family was here, from aunts and uncles to distant cousins, even some of Aunt Evelyne's friends and co-workers.

"Amelia, darling. I'm so glad you could make it back. I'm sorry if you had other plans this weekend." Her mother had found her and pulled her into a hug. Amelia could hear her sniffling behind her, and her heart warmed.

"Hey, Mom. Of course. I wouldn't miss this for the world. How's Dad doing?"

"He's been better. He was very close with his sister, and after losing your grandfather earlier this year, it's just a little much for him to handle at the moment. Jason's out back comforting him."

"I miss her, Mom. I miss her so much!" Amelia suddenly broke out in tears and wrapped her arms around her mother, crying into her shoulder and making her dress wet.

"It's okay, honey. It's okay. Your aunt only wanted what's best for all of us. She just wanted us to be happy. As long as you're happy, she's happy." Then she pulled away. "I have to finish getting everything ready. Are you okay on your own for a bit?"

Amelia nodded and watched as her mother walked upstairs.

When she turned around and walked back into the living room, where the crowd was, she noticed the back of a familiar figure.

"Alistair," she whispered. She walked up behind him and said, "Hey."

He turned around, and even during a time of sadness and sorrow, he still shone a glimmer of hope in his eyes. "Amelia, it's good seeing you again," he said, and he leaned in for a light hug.

"Yeah... hey, do you think we can step outside for a bit and talk? In private?"

Alistair glanced down at his watch before nodding. "Sure, we still have some time before we have to head out."

He followed suit as Amelia led him outside onto the patio. It wasn't the best location, with friends and family still circulating in and out through the front door, but Jason and her father had the backyard occupied, and Amelia would rather not have them eavesdrop on her conversation with Alistair.

"What's up?" he asked, sitting down on the wooden bench in front of the house. "Is everything okay? Are you okay?"

"Yeah... I-I'm fine. I just... I just... I just..." Amelia stuttered her words and began crying, sniffing though her nostrils and trying to keep herself from completely breaking down.

"Hey, hey, it's okay." Alistair pulled Amelia in closer to him, her head leaning against his chiseled chest. She could smell the old spice and vanilla cologne that she'd been so used to and so in love with during their time together, and it only brought back memories of how happy she'd been with him. "Whatever it is, I'm here, okay? I'm here. Just let it all out."

"I'm in love with you!" Amelia suddenly shouted. Luckily, no one else was around in that moment, and the chatter inside the home was too loud for anyone to pick up anything.

"What?"

"There, I said it! I'm in love with you, Alistair. And I'm sorry it took me this long to figure it out. And I'm especially sorry for pushing you away and running off during our last date. But I've tried not thinking about you. I've tried going back to my old life. I've even tried distractions, many of which I don't even wanna tell you. But Alistair, you've treated me like no one else ever had. You see me, and you're there for me no matter how much I fuck up." Amelia took a deep breath and wiped away her tears. "Aunt Evelyne was right, and it sucks that she's no longer here to see her wish come true. But I love you, Alistair. You really *are* the perfect match for me."

"Amelia, I—" Alistair began.

"You don't have to say anything now," she interrupted him. "I just needed to get it out there. I needed you to know before it's too late." She put a finger up to his lips, but he gently pushed it away.

"Amelia, I do like you. And for a while, I thought it was love that I felt, too. But watching you push me away, rejecting me, and then now this complete change, it's making me feel a little cautious. You remind me a lot of my ex. Beautiful, fun, but also impulsive. I fear that you don't know what you want. And I fear that one day, you're either going to just walk away or get yourself into an accident that you can't recover from."

"W-What are you saying, Alistair?" Amelia's voice trembled as she spoke, and even though she asked, she knew where the conversation was headed.

"I think you need to figure out what it is you really want before anything can happen between us. I care about you, Amelia, and I only want what's best for you. You'll never be happy in a relationship if you don't know what it is you're seeking." He leaned over and kissed her on her left cheek. "We should head back inside."

OVER THE NEXT FEW DAYS, Amelia found herself fighting with her own thoughts. She thought she wanted Alistair. In fact, she was so sure of it. But then again, she also said the same about David and Lucas. Maybe she wanted all of them. Or maybe she wanted none. But either way, she didn't know where to begin finding her answer.

She was back on campus, and only a month away from the realization that she'd be locked up in school all summer for failing while the rest of her classmates got to go on vacation. Things couldn't possibly get any worse.

"How'd it go with Alistair?" Melody asked, taking a sip of her smoothie.

The spring afternoon was cozy and warm, but even the fresh air wasn't enough to snap Amelia out of her slump.

"Not so great," she answered, tossing a bread crumb over to a pack of pigeons and watching them fight over it. "He doesn't want me."

"You're kidding! I thought he really liked you!"

"Yeah, I thought so, too. But when I told him how I felt, when I told him that I love him, he rejected me."

Melody shook her head. "Wow, I can't believe what I'm hearing. What an ass!"

"No," Amelia corrected her. "He's not the ass. I am. He only rejected me because he said I was being unfair to myself, letting myself get into a relationship without really knowing what I wanted."

"Well, is he right? Do you know what you want?"

"I want him. God, Mel, I just can't stop thinking about him, dreaming about him. How do I get him back?"

"Simple, Lia, you gotta just tell him, straight from the heart. If Alistair sounds like the man that you've made him out to be, I'm sure he'll understand." She checked her phone. "Listen, I have to get going. Kyle's coming over, and we're going out to dinner."

"Have fun," Amelia mumbled. And when Melody left, she pulled out her phone and dialed Alistair's number.

The ring tone was deafening when, even after the sixth try, there was no answer. She tried again, and again, and again, only to be met with that same god-awful, gut-wrenching tone.

"I lost him. I had him, the perfect man, right at the tips of my fingers, and I just pushed him away. And now, now I'm never getting him back. I deserve it," she whispered to herself and slowly trudged back to her dorm.

But when she arrived back at her building, she saw him, none other than Alistair himself!

"W-W-What are you doing here?" Amelia stuttered in surprise. "I-I tried calling you."

Alistair smiled, that same charming grin that had Amelia swooning the first time she saw it. "I know, and I'm sorry for not picking up. I wanted to surprise you."

"And you did! What are you doing here?" she asked again.

"To ask you to marry me."

"Wait, what? Really?"

Then he burst into laughter.

"You tease!" Amelia shouted.

"I'm sorry. I thought it'd be funny, given our history. But I *did* come here to ask you out, on a real date, not a setup."

"You drove all the way up here just to ask me out on a date?"

"I sure did, and I'd do it again any day. So, what do you say? Will you go out with me, Amelia Ainsworth?"

She didn't say anything back. Instead, she jumped up, wrapped her arms around his neck, and kissed him lovingly on the lips. His mouth tasted so good, his tongue so passionately dancing in her mouth, and she didn't want to pull away.

"Wait, but I thought you didn't want anything to do with me until I figured things out, until I figured out what I wanted," Amelia asked when she pulled away.

"I thought that's what would be best for us. I didn't want us rushing into anything until we're both completely certain. But every day without you felt like I was missing a piece of myself, and I hadn't realized how much I actually do love you until you said it back. So, the hell with my dumb idea. We both love each other, so let's just be with each other!" He bent down and kissed her again, wrapping his arms around her waist and tilting her head back. "So, where would you like to go? Anywhere you want."

Amelia thought about it for a minute, her finger tapping

against her chin. "There's this new arcade near here that I've been dying to go to. What do you say we make it our first *official* date?"

The End

Three Dates

Murder in Miami

TROUBLED GIRLS FIND LOVE

Murder in Miami

Murder in Miami Blurb

Who would've ever thought that a small-town girl from West Virginia would end up in prison?

Certainly not me.

And certainly not Dawson, the brooding bad boy who stole my virginity.

But not my heart.

No, that belongs to someone other than the man I'm supposed to be faithful to.

Ross. The new kid in school.

He's perfect for me in every way, but he's **not** my boyfriend.

And I can't choose!

One thing leads to another, and my entire life changes forever.

Chapter One

"Amber, please! Don't do this! I beg you; don't do this!"
"Shut up! Shut up!" His voice sounded like nails down a chalkboard inside my ears, and if I'd had my second cup of coffee this morning, I may have just been a little more lenient. But I'm tired. I'm so tired of all the games, of all the lies, of the fucking ultimatum. "Just shut up, and let me think!"

I didn't plan for this to happen. Hell, I didn't even think I'd show up. Throwing on my pajamas and climbing into bed was my way of saying "no way in hell." I thought that if I slept through the night, I'd wake up the next morning scar-free.

But instead, somehow, I found my way here, holding a gun in my hand and aiming it at the man I once loved.

"Please, Amber. I'm sorry. For everything! You don't have to do this." His voice continued to stab against my brain, and every word felt like someone was ripping off a fucking nerve.

"I don't have to do this? I don't have to do this?! The nerve of you even saying that after what you've put me through, and now you have the audacity to ask me to stop?" I found myself yelling at him, my voice growing louder and louder by the second.

To be honest, I didn't even know why I'd been so angry. And if you asked, I couldn't pinpoint the exact moment when the words that came out of his mouth turned into a bullet straight through his head. But it did.

And as I found myself trying to vigorously shake the anguish and stabbing pain out from my brain, I also found myself staring into my former lover's eyes, blood dripping from his mouth, followed by his body collapsing onto the ground and the shrieking scream of a female's voice.

Wait? Who else was here? I thought we were the only ones. Then who the fuck was yelling like a banshee that had just taken a knife to the heart?

Oh, right. Now I remember. It's my voice. I was the one screaming like a banshee.

"I killed him," I whisper to the two older men standing in front of me, tears dripping onto the handcuffs that tightly wrap around my wrists. "I killed him!"

The metal bars slam shut as they thrust me inside a cold, dark cell, with nothing but a narrow bed and what resembled half a toilet bowl keeping me company. I turn around, screaming after the men as they begin to walk away.

"Wait! I... I can't stay here! I have to see him. I have to tell him I'm sorry!" I wrap my fingers around the metal bars, gripping with all the strength I could possibly muster, shaking it back and forth and screaming for the two men to come back.

"Should've thought of that before you shot him," one of them yells back from a distance, the echo bouncing off the walls.

Shot him. Yeah, I did that alright.

JUNIOR YEAR WAS SUPPOSED to be the greatest year of my high school career... at least, that's what my parents told me when we moved all the way to Miami from our little town of Green Bank.

"You'll make friends!" she said.

"You'll have fun," he said.

She said, he said. They're all a bunch of lies.

Let me tell you this. When a parent tells you that you're the image of perfection, that you'll go far in life, that you'll never fail, they're full of shit. This fairytale world didn't exist in my little bubble of hell called "junior year." Otherwise, I wouldn't be shriveled up in nothing but my gym shorts and a granny's bra, shielding myself from the bucket full of trash that was being hurled at me from a hundred feet away.

"What's wrong, loser?" That's Cindy, head of the cheerleading team. She had locks smooth as silk and glossy as gold, the complete opposite of my tangled mess of greasy, split ends, and now, wads of gum. "You want your mommy?" She burst out into laughter along with her little posse beside her, her perky tits flopping up into the air, and her flawless face without even a single wrinkle as she continued enjoying her amusement at my demise.

To this day, I still don't know why she decided to target me like that. I wasn't special or different. I didn't get better grades than her, and I certainly wasn't more attractive than her. It was like she's Cinderella, and I'm the ugly stepsister—always the bridesmaid, never the bride.

I was a nobody, and she had everything. A rich dad, a sports car, the hottest guy in school with a smoldering look that could make anybody wet.

Why me?

"That's enough, ladies! That's enough!" That's Karen Burgundy, the gym teacher.

Everyone calls her by her first name because she'd told us that it made her seem bitchier, and no one wants to mess with a bitch. She's a widow... five times, to be exact. And she'd always tell us that her exes are no longer here because they didn't listen to her. We all thought she was just joking at first, but then it became obvious that something was just off about her. Even so, no one dared to ever investigate. They didn't want to become victim number six.

"Oh, Karen," Cindy spoke back. "We're just having a little fun! Aren't we, Amber?" She looked over at me, a look on her face that said nothing but, "I'm gonna kill you if you don't follow along."

I shivered, not from the cold air rushing through the open window that was now blowing onto my half-naked body, but from the genuine fear of what that girl is capable of doing to me.

"I... I..." She glares at me again. This time, discreetly tossing the tampon applicator she had in her hand over at me without Karen noticing. "I... Yeah, we're just having fun."

"Cindy! Into my office. Now!" Apparently, she *had* noticed.

"What the hell? She said she's having fun!" Cindy retorted, crossing her arms over chest and tucking them under her breasts.

"I said, now!" Karen wasn't having it, and as terrifying as I thought Cindy was, she was nothing compared to the angry wrath of Karen Burgundy.

"Ugh, fine! I bet all your exes killed themselves, just so they could get away from you."

A series of oohs and ahs sounded in the locker room as Karen marched over toward Cindy, snatched her wrist, and pulled her out the door. The other girls all whipped out their phones to record the whole fiasco, but it wasn't like this was anything new. Cindy was always mouthing off to the teachers.

But if anyone could. It's her. Not everyone's father can contribute billions of dollars to their kid's school.

I reached up to grab the window sill above my head once everyone had left, struggling to pull myself up from off the ground. My knees were bruised from when they'd kicked me, throwing on the sandals made from stone they all had stored in the locker before wailing against my legs. I assumed they were made from stone. Certainly felt like it.

When I finally made my way over to my own locker and opened it, I was so unsurprised that I wasn't even mad. Of course, they'd taken all my clothes. Of course, I'd have to now walk around in shorts that looked like my grandma's knickers and a bra that's meant for a maiden in the eighteen hundreds.

Just my luck. Junior year is really shaping up, Mom, just like you said.

I hugged my books against my chest as I made my way down the hall and out to the bus stop. Thank fuck that phys ed was my last class of the day. I definitely didn't want to linger around here any longer than I had to, especially almost nude.

A hundred feet remaining to the double doors. Eighty feet. Fifty feet left. Almost there.

"Hey, Amber!" Shit, that voice. The very voice that continues to haunt my dreams every night.

I turned around, and there was Cindy, dressed in her cheerleading uniform and surrounded by both the cheerleading and football teams. She certainly was the head honcho, but it makes me think if she'd end up just like me without all her loyal fans.

"You fucking got me detention for a week! A week! AND my dad canceled my party this weekend." The crowd around her booed as she continued. "You better watch your back, you little cunt. One way or another, I'll get my revenge." Then she pulled out a pair of scissors from her little Hello Kitty backpack and snipped the straps off my bra.

"What the hell did you do that for?!" I shrieked as I hurried to gather myself from being exposed to the entire school. Everyone just stood there, laughing at me, and in that moment, I felt so vulnerable with my bare back exposed for everyone to see.

"Snitches get stitches," was all Cindy could say before taking out her phone and pressing record.

"I didn't snitch on you! You were just too stupid to fool her!" I was shouting, but I didn't know why. I didn't want payback against her; I just wanted to run home, lock myself in the closet, and never come out again.

"Well," Cindy chuckled, "at least I'm not the one in my underwear."

"What?"

And less than a second later, I found my gym shorts being torn in half and falling onto the ground. Laundry day wasn't until later that night, and I'd been ashamed even at home to wear my purple and green polka dot granny panties. Now I found myself sporting them like I was a model prancing down the runway.

"Hey, everyone, look! Amber the Snitch here wears her mom's underwear! So embarrassing!" Then Cindy leaned in closer. "Maybe if you'd spend less time snitching and more time at the mall, you wouldn't be such an outcast!"

I wanted to yell back, scream at her even, spit in her face. But I knew I had been defeated. Anything else I threw her way would only act as ammo against me, and simply leaving was the best thing I could do for myself.

I forced myself to hold back my tears as I clutched the books closer to me and ran out the doors. Screw the bus stop. I didn't live that far from school. I'd have better luck not being seen just running home instead. Undergarments and sneakers weren't exactly the trendiest look, but if Regina George can pull of such hideous fashion, why couldn't I?

I was less than two blocks from home when I collided into something, or someone, who would eventually change my life forever.

Chapter Two

"Whoa, easy there—" The man who ran into me stopped mid-speech and looked me up and down, his face quickly turning a bright shade of pink. "You're... You're—"

"I know!" I shouted, bending over to gather my belongings and quickly covering my bare chest back up.

"But... why? You work in a strip club or something? A little young, but I suppose—"

I peered at him closer as he spoke. He was definitely trying too hard to pull off that bad boy look. I mean, a leather jacket AND spikes? Not to mention the very unflattering half-lit cigarette that was dangling from in between his lips. Sure, I despised the cheerleaders and the jocks, but his type was right up there also on my list of losers to stay away from.

"Are you serious?" I cut him off. "What kind of stripper carries around a thick ass textbook on Trigonometry?"

"One who's trying not to completely disappoint her father?" he teased, batting an eye at me.

I cringed, but let my guard down. Then I remembered that I was no longer covering myself up, and I was completely flashing this stranger standing in front of me. I quickly raced my arms back up, crossing them over my chest. "I have to go."

"Wait!" He called out to me and grabbed onto one of my arms, catching me off-guard and causing me to drop my books and expose my bare breasts to this strange man once again.

"What the fuck, dude?" I yelled out to him. "Why can't you just leave me alone?"

"I'm... I'm sorry. I didn't mean to do that. I just wanted to know your name."

"Why?" My face was growing hot with fury, but my heart was also beginning to warm up. For a bad boy, he looked pretty cute when he's all ashamed and timid.

"Because I think you're really pretty." His eyes traveled down to the lower half of my body, and as I caught him staring straight at green and purple polka dots, he said, "Even if you *are* sporting a Barney-inspired look."

"If you're just gonna insult me, I may as well just be on my way. Is that the only reason you stopped me?"

"What? No, I never got a chance to introduce myself. I'm Dawson, by the way." He extended his hand out, but I refused to do the same.

"Amber," I answered him, "and I'd shake your hand, under different circumstances."

"Oh, right. My bad." He withdrew his hand back and ran a few fingers through his hair. "It's nice to meet you, Amber. Such a pretty name. Here, take my jacket. It'll cover you up a bit more." As I watched him take the leather jacket off his back, I couldn't help but stare at those delicious biceps that he'd been hiding beneath it.

I grabbed the jacket from him, temporarily placing my textbooks down on the ground and showing my boobs to the whole town, Dawson included, so I could throw it over my shoulders. Luckily, it was long enough to cover even my polka dot butt, and I no longer needed to use Trigonometry as my own personal wardrobe.

"Thanks, you have no idea the day I've had." I thanked him, finally extending my hand for a handshake. "You're literally a lifesaver."

"Ha-ha, I can imagine. It's not every day I see a girl running around in her underwear." Then he winked. "Not that I'm complaining."

"My house is only a couple blocks away. If you wanna walk with me, I can give you your jacket back after I put on something decent." I gestured over to my right, waiting for him to accept the invitation and follow me.

"Nah," he simply said.

"Nah...? Do you want it back now? But I just—"

He laughed again. "Of course not, silly! I meant 'nah' as in, if I take it back now, how else am I going to see you again?"

Clever. I like it, but a bit odd. I've never been someone to attract men. Sure, I'd been pretty back in Green Bank, but with a population of under two hundred and most of the girls there dressed in hay and manure, I didn't have much competition. But here? These Miami supermodels make me look like one of them had just crapped me out after a good night at Taco Bell.

"You mean a date?" I asked him.

I'm not stupid. I knew that's what he was reaching for, but I was loving the attention, and the more flattery I could get from someone, the better.

"No, I mean I wanna get you all alone in a warehouse so I could put a bullet through your head. Of course, I mean a date!"

That was oddly specific. I wondered if this meeting was even accidental. Maybe he'd been roaming the streets of Miami for weeks, scouting out unsuspecting girls whom he could kidnap and take back to his little dungeon to murder. Maybe I was walking into my own death.

I had half a mind to turn around and run away, taking his jacket with me and putting in a restraining order for the sake of my own life, but then I looked into his eyes, and fuck, I'm such a sucker for those puppy-dog eyes. So, I gave in.

"Fine." I sighed. "Where're we going?"

"Tomorrow night at six. We'll meet again here. It'll be our special spot." Then he winked at me and walked away.

I sighed, wrapping the jacket around me so it snugged around my thin frame. I didn't even notice myself blushing until the heat started emanating from my face. Dawson. Miami might not be so bad after all.

THE NEXT EVENING, I made sure to show up properly dressed, though I'm sure I would've become his favorite woman if I hadn't. I didn't have much—moving from such a small town where my parents didn't have much, and the girls I hung around cared more about their studies than a competition of who's the sexiest in town.

But Miami was humid! And I knew I needed to sport something other than sweatpants and a shaggy sweater. So, I pulled out an old pair of jeans, and with my trusty pair of scissors, I turned it into frayed shorts. I then threw a baggy t-shirt over the top half of my body and tied a knot on the back so it looked more fitting.

"Wow, I didn't expect to see you with so much clothes on," Dawson teased when I met him at the spot. Honestly, even a minute of standing there began to bring back horrific memories of the day before, but the sun had set, and being so new to the city, luckily not very many people would recognize me.

"I could say the same about you." I grinned, looking up and down his all-leather look. "Do you own anything else other than leather?"

He winked. "I got a few pairs of boxers. Wanna see?"

I shook my head. "I'm good."

"Ha! Good, cause I ain't wearing any."

"Do you always joke around like that?" I asked him, rolling my eyes at his poor sense of humor.

"Who's joking? I actually like going commando every once in a while. It's actually very freeing. You should try it some time." He raised a brow at me. "You know, what you were doing yesterday, but the... opposite?"

"Very funny. Not!" I crossed my arms over my chest. "Is that why you asked me to come out here tonight? So you could humiliate me even more than I've already been?" Then I threw my hands up in the air. "God! I knew my family should've never moved here. Miami is full of nothing but a shitty bunch of—"

And before I could even register what was happening, Dawson was kissing me. He'd grabbed me by the shoulders, spun me around, and planted his full lips against mine, massaging both my lips and tongue like he was kneading a roll of dough with his mouth.

Kissing strangers weren't my thing. Never have been. But when someone as hot as Dawson, with lips made of magic, starts kissing you, you'd be a fool to not kiss back. So warm. So inviting. Like we've been doing this for years, and this kiss signified the start of the rest of our lives together.

"So, what were you saying?" he asked with a grin when we pulled away. "Miami is full of nothing but a shitty bunch of...?"

"I... I... I don't remember."

"That's what I thought." Then he leaned in and kissed me again.

Chapter Three

I'd been dating Dawson for a little short of six months now, and my reputation in school had skyrocketed to superstar levels. I went from being the loser, new girl running around in her underwear to the most popular girl in school, with her hot arm candy by her side. Even Cindy and her gang of plastic dolls started to treat me like I was someone famous! Inviting me to sit with them at lunch and even go shopping with them after school at the mall.

I didn't know who I was anymore, but I wasn't sure if I liked who I was becoming. I'd never been one to have so much popularity around me, and my roots of growing up as a small-town girl were beginning to fade.

I liked Dawson. I really did. And there's a ninety percent chance that I'm not just saying that because he took my virginity.

Yeah, I said it. About a week after our first kiss, I gave in. We weren't even officially dating yet, and that had only been my second time seeing him. But he said all the right things. Told me the words that every teenage girl wanted to hear.

I love you.

He said it! Not me. Well, not at first.

But then I found myself sitting in his car, his hand sliding up my skirt as he kissed me first on my lips, and then slowly down my neck, and the next thing I knew, he was leaning the passenger seat of the car back and climbing on top of me.

"I want you, Amber," he whispered into my ear, sliding his hand further and further up until I felt chills course through my body.

I didn't stop him. In fact, I wasn't even completely sure what to do in that moment. He was the first boy I'd ever been with, and I had no concept of what "moving too fast" meant. So, I just tilted my head back and closed my eyes, letting both his hands and tongue roam around my body—his mouth encircling my breasts, and his bare hips swaying against mine —and when I felt something hard and warm enter inside of me, I gasped.

"It's okay. I'll take good care of you. I promise." Then he kissed me again, thrusting himself faster and faster, deeper and deeper, until a loud sound escaped from his lips, and he collapsed on top of me.

"I love you," he whispered into my ear.

"I love you, too."

And now, I was beginning to second guess whether I had actually meant what I'd said, or whether the first orgasm I'd ever experienced sent me so far over the edge that I was even willing to say those same three words to a pigeon waddling down the street.

"Hey, babe. I'll catch you after school. Gotta go take care of some things." Dawson pulled me out of my thoughts and gave me a kiss on the cheek.

I flashed him a light smile as he started walking off with a few of his buddies, barely even registering my response. It didn't seem like he really cared, anyway. Hell, I didn't really care. Dawson was way out of my league, and whether he's with me for me or as arm candy, I'll never really know.

However, as I turned back around, a glaring light blinded my eyes, and it took me a second before I noticed the face in it. A boy, brown hair, and glasses that seemed just a little too large for his face. But he reminded me of the boys I used to know back in Green Bank, the down-to-earth homebodies that I'd grown up with.

And he was new. Well, at least to me, he was. But to me, half the school was still new. Despite everyone knowing me, I'd become enclosed in my little circle I liked to call "Dawson and I."

"Hey, four eyes! Watch where you're going!" I heard behind me as I turned back to my locker to grab my books for next period.

When I turned to face the boy again, I saw Dawson and his buddies knocking into him, pushing him around before eventually kicking him to the ground and walking away laughing. I liked Dawson, but he could be a real ass sometimes. However, I guess it was good to have someone like him on my side. Otherwise, I'd probably be scrambling around the ground for my things also.

But my heart felt for him. It felt like it was just yesterday when I found myself crouched down inside the locker room, bombarded by Cindy and her gang. It's never easy being the new kid. The least I could do was help him.

I walked over and picked up a book, Introduction to Electromagnetism. "Here, I think this belongs to you." I crouched down and handed it over to him.

A timid look glared up at me, and I could see the thin blue ring around his dark brown eyes. How unique.

"Yeah, thanks." He gave me a weak smile and gathered the rest of his things before standing back up. I followed, the textbook still in my hands.

"Electromagnetism, huh? Sounds difficult. You must be really smart."

But he just raised his brows at me and grabbed the book from me when I extended my hand. "Come on, we both know that's not the reason you came over here. To tell me that I'm smart."

He really is smart. "You're right. I saw how those guys treated you, and I just wanted to apologize on their behalf. I know what it's like being the new kid. I thought I'd help you out a little."

"I don't need anyone's pity. And why are you apologizing for them? You know them or something?"

My face turned red. "I... I... no. I don't. I just know they're a bunch of bullies, and you didn't deserve that."

"Thanks. Name's Ross, by the way." He extended his hand out to me.

"Amber."

"Is today your first day also, Amber?

I shook my head. "I've actually been here for about six months now. Still getting the hang of things, though. I'm originally from Green Bank—"

"West Virginia?"

I nodded.

"No way! I'm from Dunmore! I just moved here last week!"

"Wow," I chuckled, "and here I was thinking I'm the odd one out."

"I guess we can now *both* be weirdos together." He chuckled back. Suddenly, the bell rang. He turned to me and waved. "Well, gotta get over to, you know," he pointed at his textbook and then behind him, "this and all. Gotta keep up the grades. You know how it is."

"Yeah, uh, sure." I didn't, not really. I'd never been into

school or getting straight As, but he was definitely the type to care.

"Hey, this might be a little too forward, but would you be interested in grabbing some ice cream with me after school? I don't know much about this chaos of a city, and it'd be great to have a fellow West Virginian show me around."

I paused. I'd promised Dawson I'd meet up with him at the arcade after school. Him and his buddies were going to attempt to beat a new game that had just released, and he needed me there for emotional support.

But I'd also just made a friend, someone I could actually connect with. Did I really want to give that up for a game?

"Sure." I smiled at Ross. "I'd love to."

"Great! See you in about...," he looked down at his watch, "two hours and thirty-six minutes! It's a date!"

I pushed my way out through the double doors of the front entrance and could barely catch my breath. What the hell was I doing? Did he really just say *date*? Ugh! I mean, he's cute and all, for a shy guy, but I'm with Dawson. Was I really just about to bail on him for another dude?

Suddenly, my phone rang, and I jumped up with a mini heart attack.

"Hello?" I answered.

"Hey, babe! We still on for later? I can't wait to have my lucky charm with me as I crush this!" It was Dawson.

"Hey, don't hate me, but I was wondering if I could skip. I think I ate something bad during lunch, and now I'm not feeling too great. I think I might just go home and go straight to bed."

"Shucks, well, that blows. I was really counting on you to be there!"

"I'm sorry, babe. Next time, I promise to be there for you. I'll even wear a mini skirt and carry pom poms."

"I'd take you in a mini skirt any day, sweet cheeks. And I

don't mean your face." I didn't need to see it. He was clearly giving me his signature wink. "How about I come over after and see how you're feeling? Maybe cheer you up?"

"I'd like that. But just remember to come over after seven. That's when my mom leaves for work."

"Aw, she doesn't wanna stay for the fun?"

"Dawson!"

"I'm just messin' with you. Seven it is. I love you, babe."

"I love you, Dawson." And as I hung up, I twitched my face. I'd been saying "I love you" to him for months, but it never seemed to get any easier the more I did it.

Chapter Four

I met up with Ross at Kazoo's. It's a little further away from the city than I would've liked, but I couldn't risk Dawson finding out that I'd ditched him for another guy. Turned out, we both liked pistachio ice cream drizzled with a hefty serving of caramel sauce. I could've sworn to my grave that I was the only one who liked that combination.

"So, tell me, Amber, why'd you move to Miami? I mean, it's so different from Green Bank!" Ross mumbled in between spoonfuls to his mouth.

I shrugged. "My parents just wanted a change, I guess. My dad got a job offer that he said he couldn't turn down, but I know he'd been eyeing Miami for quite some time now, and this was just the perfect excuse to make that jump."

"But... but you don't fit in!"

"What the hell is that supposed to mean? I fit in just fine!"

"Amber, look around you."

I quickly glanced around. All the girls walking around outside were dressed like they had just come from the beach, and all the guys looked like they forgot to do this week's laundry. I guess Ross was right. I didn't exactly fit in with my purple cardigan.

Then I shook my head. "What's with the interrogation, anyway? I could ask you the same thing! It's not like you belong here anymore than I do!"

"That's the point. I don't! That's why I was so ecstatic when I found out that you're just like me. I was about ready to hop on the next bus out of town before I met you today." Ross shot me a bashful grin, a grin that said, "I know I'm not the best grape in the bunch, but please be nice to me."

And I couldn't help but release a light giggle. He wasn't Dawson, confident and brooding, but Ross was sweet, and I could really see us becoming great friends.

HOURS WENT BY, and I didn't notice how late it was getting outside until Kazoo's started smelling like detergent.

"Ah, shit! What time is it?" I glanced down at my watch. Just ten minutes before seven. Fuck. "I... I have to go." I quickly stuttered to Ross and grabbed my things, throwing down a ten-dollar bill for my ice cream before running toward the door.

"Wait!" he shouted after me. I stopped. I shouldn't have, but I did. "When can we hang out again? I had such a great time with you."

I felt my face blush. It wasn't something I thought I'd ever do with someone other than Dawson, but the way Ross looked at me just made me feel things inside. "I'm not sure. Soon?" I hesitated. "I think I might be busy for a while."

"Let me at least give you my number, in case you change your mind." I barely had a chance to stop him before he jotted his number down on a piece of napkin and tucked it into the side pocket of my backpack. Then he gave me a pat on the shoulder. "If I get the honor of hanging out with you again, then that'd be superb. If not, then I guess I'll just be that pathetic loser at school who longs after you like a puppy dog."

"That's a terrible joke." I chuckled and pushed open the door. "I'll see you around, Ross."

"See you around."

I made it back home with just enough time to throw myself into my robe and quickly shuffle up my hair. I needed to be just convincing enough so that Dawson would think I was home all night. I hated lying to him, and it wasn't even like I was doing anything wrong. But Dawson and Ross clearly didn't get along, and I bet just the mention of his name would set my boyfriend off.

A second after I washed my makeup off my face, the bell rang. I steadied myself and made my way downstairs, where I saw Dawson peering through the front window.

"Hey, babe. How're you feeling?" He handed me a bouquet of flowers when I flung the door open. "Oh! And I got you some chicken noodle. It's not homemade, but the host at the diner said it's still pretty tasty."

Fuck. Of course, he turns into the best boyfriend ever on the day I decide to betray him.

"Thanks," I gave him a soft smile, "this is all very sweet of you. You didn't have to do all this."

"Why wouldn't I? You're my girl. And I take care of my girl. So, how you feeling? Well enough to kiss?" Dawson closed the door behind him as he walked inside the house, and he drew me into a bear hug before rubbing my shoulders. "I missed you this afternoon. I crushed the game, but I definitely could've gotten a better score." He leaned in and kissed me on the cheek. "It's because I was missing my lucky charm."

"I'll be there next time, I promise. I'll make it up to you."

Then he winked at me. "Or you can just make it up to me now." And before I knew it, he scooped me up by the legs and carried me up to my room, where he lightly threw my body against the bed and hovered his own body over me, planting kisses across my neck and beginning to untie the robe.

"Dawson, wait. I'm sick, remember?" I put a hand to his chest and stopped him. But if there was one thing I knew well about Dawson, was that he didn't let anything—and I mean anything—get in the way between him and a warm, slimy hole.

"Babe, I'd rather risk getting sick than spend another day without your body pressed up against mine." Then he leaned back down and continued with the kisses.

His lips felt so warm, so dominating, that it brought me back to when we first made love, when he took my virginity. And I felt myself giving in instantly, almost forgetting where I'd really been and the reason why he was even here tonight.

I whispered a moan as he pulled his shirt over his head and came back down, reaching a hand off to one side of the bed as I nibbled on his left ear, his favorite spot. Then I heard a crinkle when he extended his reach, and memories of why that crinkle existed shot back into my thoughts.

"What's this?" He reached into the netted side pocket of my backpack and pulled out *the* crinkled sheet. And when he unfolded it, my heart dropped. "Who the *fuck* is Ross?" His bellow almost shot through my ceiling with how loud it sounded, and he climbed off the bed to throw his shirt back on.

"What? No one!" I fumbled to come up with a decent enough lie. "Just a friend from school."

"Amber, come on. I know who your friends are, and you definitely don't know someone named Ross. Besides, what kind of friend draws a heart next to their number?"

"Umm, a cheeky one?"

"Amber! Are you fucking cheating on me?"

"No!" I jumped off the bed and grabbed him by the

hands, squeezing them tight in hopes that it'd quell his anger enough for me to explain myself.

"Then explain this!"

"He's just a friend! I swear! He moved here from my state, and we just got to talking. But we didn't do anything! We just went out for ice cream." God, I wish I could take back my words sometimes.

"Today? Is that why you ditched me? To hang out with some other guy? Were you even sick?" I bowed my head and slowly shook it. "You're unbelievable, Amber! I give you nothing but love, and you go behind my back with some other dude?"

"Well, you never even asked if I wanted to spend my day at the arcade."

"That doesn't give you an excuse to cheat on me!"

"I wasn't—" He was gone before I could say anything else, slamming his way out of my bedroom, down the stairs, and out the front door.

Chapter Five

It'd been three days since our fight, and Dawson refused to pick up any of my calls. Even when I'd see him at school and call out his name, he'd just run in the opposite direction, forever giving me the cold shoulder.

"Give him time," one of his buddies told me once. "He just needs some time to think. He loves you. He'll come around."

And I would've believed him had it not been for Cindy and her fat mouth.

"You look particularly happy today. Something happen?" I overheard Megan, one of Cindy's clones, on the third day asking her by the lockers. I backed up an inch and hid behind the water fountain. Nearly half the school knew about Dawson and my fight, and I couldn't deal with any more drama than I already was.

"Well, Meg, generally, I don't kiss and tell, but if you must know. I had sex." Cindy sung.

"I don't get it. You and Jordan have sex all the time. Isn't it like... your thing?"

"Ah, but that's the best part." She leaned in closer to her

friend, but I could still hear every word. "It wasn't with Jordan."

"You cheated—?"

"Shh, tell the whole school, will ya?"

"Then who?"

Cindy smirked. "Dawson."

I felt my heart immediately drop down to my stomach as I stood there frozen, listening to Cindy describe every detail—from the way he encircled her fake breasts with his tongue, to the way he played with her until she couldn't contain herself anymore, to the way he inserted himself into her bare body as if they were two pieces of a jigsaw puzzle.

So, that's why he didn't answer my calls? Because he was fucking Cindy?

I couldn't breathe, and I definitely couldn't stand there for another second listening to Cindy tell the whole school how big my boyfriend's dick was. I had to get out of here. I had to go. I had to—

I spun myself around and bolted for the double doors. I could feel my whole world around me suffocating me, and I didn't know how much longer I could contain myself before passing out onto the ground. And I didn't stop until I made my way out into the school parking lot and collapsed into myself. My stupid parents should've never left Green Bank. I was just fine where I was in my cushy lifestyle.

"Amber?"

I spun my head toward the voice and saw none other than Ross himself walking toward me. Tears were still heavily flowing down my cheeks, and I quickly rushed to wipe them away before he could realize that I'd been crying.

"Ross," I managed to choke out, "wh-what are you doing here?"

"I saw you run out while heading to bio and wanted to

check in on you. You okay?" Then he peered closer at me. "Looks like you'd been crying."

Damn. He noticed.

"I-I'm fine. Just allergies."

Ross shook his head. "I get allergies like crazy, and I can spot one from a mile away. This isn't it. Besides, if you don't tell me, I can always easily find out myself. I'm a genius, remember?"

I drew a slight grin from his joke, then I sighed. Time to spill the tea.

"It's Dawson. You know, the one who bullied you? He's actually my boyfriend." I cringed, expecting to see a look of surprise on his face at the shocking news. Instead, he just shrugged, like he'd already known. "Anyway, we got into a huge fight, and he's been ignoring me for a few days now. And I just found out that he'd been sleeping with Cindy, my sworn enemy, and now it just feels like my world is falling apart."

I started sniffling again, and felt a wave of comfort wash over me when Ross pulled me in for a hug. "Don't beat yourself up over it too much. That guy's kinda an asshole, anyway. You deserve someone better."

"Why's that?"

"Huh?"

"Why's he an asshole?" I repeated.

"Well, first, he's a bully. All I ever see him do at school is get high in the boy's restroom, and you might not have noticed, but I've seen the way he treats you compared to how he treats other girls. It's almost like he's just with you because you put out."

"You've known about us?"

He shrugged. "Not that hard to put the pieces together when you two are literally the only thing anyone can talk about these days."

Why was he being so nice to me? Even after I'd lied to

him? I dropped my head down onto his shoulder when he pulled away slightly. "I'm sorry for not telling you. I didn't think you'd be my friend if I told you I was dating the guy who beat the crap out of you."

"Nah, it's cool. His actions don't define who you are. Besides, if I lost you, who else would I talk about the Mountaineers with?"

"We don't even like football!" I exclaimed and gave him a playful push.

"Heh, yeah, but I like knowing I have the option. Come on, let's go back inside. Get through this last period, and we can go watch a movie or something. Take your mind off of all this." He extended his hand out for me to take.

I nodded, grabbed his soft, baby skin hand, and together, we walked back inside... just to find Cindy's half-naked body pressed up against Dawson against the lockers, and her kissing him hard on the lips. "Jordan was never man enough for me. I'm glad I dumped his ass for you, sexy, sexy, Dawson."

"L-Let's get o-out of h-here," I stuttered and pulled Ross back toward the doors with me.

"But school isn't over yet—"

"I don't care!" I shouted, but everyone was too busy fawning over Cindy and Dawson to care.

I dropped Ross' hand, ran through the parking lot, and down the closest street. I needed to get as far away from here as possible. I needed to get away from Dawson, from Cindy, from this whole fucking city! I hated it here!

Chapter Six

I ran and ran until my legs started to feel like jelly. I stopped and leaned against a fence, catching my breath. *I should just hop on the next bus back to West Virginia and leave all this behind. My parents can stay if they want to, but no way in hell am I gonna.*

"Jesus, Amber! You're fast!" Ross panted next to me seconds later.

"You followed me?"

"Of course! I care about you. I saw what happened back there, and if I were in your shoes, I'd have done the same. I just wanted to make sure you didn't jump off a bridge or something."

I rolled my eyes. "I'm upset, not suicidal."

"Yeah, but still."

"What about last period?"

"Making sure you're okay is more important. I already have enough credits to get into college. School is just a hobby to me now."

"You really are smart, aren't you?" I asked. When he didn't respond, I followed up with, "How about that movie then?"

"I guess? Now that we're both out. But theaters won't let us in there until after three. You know, to prevent people from sneaking out of school early? Like us?"

But I shook my head. "Let's just go back to my place. My mom's working double shifts today. She won't be home for a while."

"Are you sure? I don't wanna feel like I'm intruding or anything."

"Positive."

When we got back to my house, I threw my shoes against the staircase and popped into the fridge to grab a couple beers. Dad always had way more lying around than he needed. He'd never notice a few missing here and there.

"Here," I said to Ross as I handed him one.

"Beer? Amber, we're underage!"

"So? It's not like adults are that responsible either when they drink." Truth be told, I only had my first drink after I met Dawson. He handed me a cold one after we'd made out in his car and told me it'd make me feel a lot better. I nearly threw up after my first sip, but after a while, my body started feeling looser, and it felt good to be free from my worries for even just a few minutes.

But still, he continued shaking his head, like a real party pooper.

"Humor me, would you?" I insisted and extended the bottle closer to him.

"Amber, I can't." His voice was low, like something I'd said bothered him.

"Why are you being so pathetic?" I nearly screamed at him, but I covered my mouth as soon as the words came out. "I-I'm so sorry. I don't know why I said that."

"You're just upset, Amber. I get it. First, your boyfriend cheats on you, and now the one thing you want from me, you can't have."

"Why won't you just drink one? Even a couple sips?"

Ross' face fell, his shoulders slack. "It's not that I don't want to. It's that I can't. I've had alcohol before, Amber, and it does nothing but mess me up. I just don't wanna risk doing something I might regret, especially when I'm not inside my own home."

"Something you'd regret? Like what? You're the goodiest two-shoes I know!"

His face turned red as he blushed, his hands rubbing together like he was about to sweat bullets. "Something like kissing you."

I froze in place. "What?" *Had I heard that right?*

"Amber, I've liked you since I first met you, but since you were with Dawson, I couldn't do anything about it. So, I just friend-zoned myself, if that meant I could still hang out with you. But I hope you now understand why I can't take anything that'll screw up those inhibitions."

Hell, why was I still lying to myself? It wasn't like I hadn't felt the same way about Ross. We just seemed to fit better together than Dawson and I—whom I had absolutely nothing in common with. And he'd been there for me when all Dawson could do was ignore me and go behind my back with Cindy. What, are they dating now? Is it over between Dawson and I? Is that why he was *kissing* her?

I didn't give myself much time to think before I leaned over and pressed my face against Ross', taking him off-guard as he jumped back in surprise. I didn't want anything to stop me from doing what I was about to do.

"Whoa, whoa, Amber, hold up. You have a boyfriend." Ross shifted back in his seat and slowly inched away.

"Do I, though? Or is he out there cheating on me? And why are you against this? You literally just told me you liked me!"

"I do. I really do, but this doesn't feel right to me. You're in a vulnerable position, and I don't want to take advantage of you."

"But what if I told you I like you, too? More than I like Dawson."

"Amber, I don't know…"

But I leaned back in regardless, caressing his face against my hands and slowly moving my lips toward his. "Shh, don't say that. I want you, Ross, and I know you want me, too, so why are we fighting this?" I softly placed my lips over his and could taste the peppermint from his ChapStick, massaging first his upper lip, then his lower, with my own, and soon, I felt hands wrapping around my waist.

He leaned me back against the couch and continued to kiss me, wrapping me in his arms as if he were holding something precious that he didn't ever want to let go of. His kisses were gentle and meaningful, the complete opposite of Dawson's slobbery ones that always seemed to drench my face.

I reached behind him and slowly lifted his shirt while he continued to hold me dearly.

"Are you sure you want to do this?" he whispered into my ear, and when I nodded, he proceeded to take his shirt off for me. And his body, wow! It didn't look like Dawson's, with his muscular build and glaringly obvious tattoos, but Ross was jacked in his own right, and I definitely didn't mind the abs that were staring me in the face.

Then I felt his hands slide up my skirt cautiously, as it seemed he wanted to avoid whatever was going to sneak out and bite his fingers off. And as he did, he continued to kiss my chest, sliding the straps of my tank top off my shoulders and kissing lower and lower until…

My phone rang. I reached over to see who it was as Ross continued to plant kisses along the top of my breasts, his hands reaching higher and higher until I felt a shivering sensation shoot up my body.

It was Dawson. *What? Is he calling just to tell me how great Cindy's boobs are?*

I slapped the phone back down and let my thoughts wander through my brain. What was I doing? About to have sex with a guy I'd only just met? I lied there, still, for a moment while Ross continued to kiss me. The feelings of pleasure and revenge that I'd felt mere minutes ago were beginning to turn into guilt and regret, and I pushed Ross off of me.

"Why'd you do that?" he asked, clutching onto his left elbow. Must've fallen on his shoe or something.

"I-I'm sorry, Ross. I can't do this. You have to go."

"But I thought we were—"

"You have to go! Now!" I shouted and proceeded to throw his shoes out the door. Like a puppy who had just been kicked, he grabbed his shirt off the couch and walked out after them.

After I slammed the door behind him, I picked the unopened bottle of beer up off the table and threw it against the wall. The glass shattered, and the dark liquid oozed down the white paint, staining everything in its path as it dripped down to the floor. I screamed, louder than I'd ever screamed before, and I didn't care whether any of the neighbors heard.

I hated myself! I hated the life I was living! I'd been so optimistic about starting a new school in a new city, but this fucking town was full of nothing but fakes. Deceptive fakes who do nothing but use you and then screw you over.

"I hate you, Dawson!!"

Then my phone dinged. A text. I slowly dragged myself over to where I'd left my phone and picked it up.

Dawson.

DAWSON

Hey, can we talk?

I typed back.

AMBER

No.

DAWSON

Well, you don't really have much of a choice. I'm outside.

Chapter Seven

S hit! Did he see Ross? Did he see... us? I felt my body shaking aggressively as I stumbled over to the door. I peered through the side window of the front door, and there he was, waving at me. Now I *had* to open it.

I flung open the door, expecting Dawson to fume with anger, but he had his hands in his pockets and shuffled his feet on the door mat.

"Can I come in?" he asked.

I nodded and stepped off to the side. Everything felt so different now, so... awkward. The last time he'd been here, I leapt into his arms and made out with him on my bed. Now, I struggled just meeting him eye-to-eye.

"I saw Ross leaving your house."

Crap. He did see him. Did they talk? Does he know what I did?

"Well, what do you care? You fucked Cindy!" I didn't know why I was screaming. I hadn't meant to, but my frustration with everyone around me just sent me over the edge, and I didn't quite know how to dial it back.

"What the hell are you talking about?

"Cindy! It's all over school. You fucked her!" I yelled again.

"What?! Are you insane? No, I didn't!"

"But she said—"

"Amber! I don't care what she said. Who are you gonna believe? Your boyfriend, or someone who hates your guts enough to ruin it?" The look in Dawson's eyes were genuine, like he had nothing to hide.

"Then how do you explain her kissing you? By the lockers today?"

"You mean the kiss that she just threw on me? And if you'd watched a bit longer, you would've seen me pushing her away. Why are you interrogating me, anyway? You're the one who had another guy over."

"Wait, did you say you're still my boyfriend?"

"Yeah, were you fucking another dude?" The anger was starting to grow in his voice.

"So, does that mean Cindy made all that up? You never did anything with her?"

"Amber, if I did, wouldn't I be with her right now instead of standing here?" I stayed silent. "Are you gonna tell me what happened with Ross?"

"We're... we're just friends. That's all." I stuttered while trying to get those words out, and even I didn't believe what I had said.

"Bullshit, Amber. No guy wants to be just friends with a girl without wanting something more. Did you two fuck?"

"No! We didn't!"

"Then why was he here? At your house? In the middle of the fucking day?"

"Because I thought you were cheating on me, so I asked him to come over to cheer me up. But nothing happened, I swear!"

But he could tell that I was lying through my teeth. I was

never any good at lying, and it became glaringly obvious the more nervous I got.

"Oh, really? Then why do you have a dude's sock on your couch?"

I looked over to where he was nodding, and staring at me right in the face, was a black sock.

"Oh, that's just my dad's."

That was a mistake. Dawson walked over to where the sock was and picked it up. And to my demise, Ross' fucking mother had stitched his name on the inside tag!

"I'm sorry!" I blurted. "We just made out, but I swear, we didn't have sex! We were about to, but then you called, and I couldn't do it anymore. So, I kicked him out!"

"Why would you do that to me? How could you cheat on me? After everything we've been through?"

"Because I thought you were cheating on me! I'm so sorry, Dawson!" I clung onto his arm like plastic wrap. I didn't think I ever loved him, but the thought of losing him felt more terrifying that spending the rest of my life with him.

But he pushed me away. "I don't know, Amber. I trusted you. I love you, for fuck's sake! And you go ahead and pull this shit?"

"Please, Dawson, please don't go! Let me make this up to you! How can I get you to forgive me?"

"Kill Ross."

AND THAT'S how I found myself standing inside this warehouse. Dawson had given me an ultimatum—kill Ross, or lose him for good. The plan was to get him out of my life for good. Eliminate the threat. It was the only way Dawson could ever stay with me.

But I didn't know how to go through with it. The plan

was to lure Ross into the warehouse, giving him whatever he needed just to get him there, and then put a bullet through his head. But as the days counted down to that moment, I felt myself flickering back and forth between the two men in my life.

On the one hand, Dawson was hot, a god if I'd ever seen one. But we had nothing in common other than the fact that he'd taken my virginity. On the other hand, Ross was everything I'd ever wanted, a small-town boy with plenty to give and the promise of never betraying me.

But I loved Dawson. He was my first, and I wanted to give him what he wanted so we could stay together. Dawson. Ross. Dawson. Ross. Who do I choose? Or do I just walk away from them both?

"Amber, please! Don't do this! I beg you; don't do this!"

"Shut up! Shut up!" His voice sounded like nails down a chalkboard inside my ears, and if I'd had my second cup of coffee this morning, I may have just been a little more lenient. But I'm tired. I'm so tired of all the games, of all the lies, of the fucking ultimatum. "Just shut up, and let me think!"

The line between what I'd done to myself and what others had done to me was beginning to blur, and even though a part of me knew that none of this was exactly his fault, I couldn't find the strength to pull myself out of my trance.

I didn't plan for this to happen. Hell, I didn't even think I'd show up. Throwing on my pajamas and climbing into bed was my way of saying "no way in hell." I thought that if I slept through the night, I'd wake up the next morning scar-free.

But instead, somehow, I found my way here, holding a gun in my hand and aiming it at the man I once loved. Maybe because I knew that if I didn't take matters into my own hands, the two of them would end up dead the next day.

"Please, Amber. I'm sorry. For everything! You don't have to do this. I'll forgive you! Just please, don't pull the trigger."

His voice continued to stab against my brain, and every word felt like someone was ripping off a fucking nerve.

"I don't have to do this? I don't have to do this?! The nerve of you even saying that after what you've put me through, and now you have the audacity to ask me to stop?" I found myself yelling at him, my voice growing louder and louder by the second.

But in reality, I was just yelling at myself. At this little voice inside my head that refused to shut up. And if I'd recognized sooner that I was only taking my anger out on him, maybe this night wouldn't have ended in a bloodbath.

To be honest, I didn't even know why I'd been so angry. And if you asked, I couldn't pinpoint the exact moment when the words that came out of his mouth turned into a bullet straight through his head. But it did. And as I found myself trying to vigorously shake the anguish and stabbing pain out from my brain, I also found myself staring into my former lover's eyes, blood dripping from his mouth, followed by his body collapsing onto the ground and the shrieking scream of a female's voice.

Wait? Who else was here? I thought we were the only ones. Then who the *fuck* was yelling like a banshee that had just taken a knife to the heart?

Oh, right. Now I remember. It's *my* voice. *I* was the one screaming like a banshee.

I looked around me, and Ross was nowhere to be found. He must've snuck out the back when Dawson was begging for his life, and after a night of emotional terror, I found myself standing in front of a lifeless body, his blood pooling around my feet, with a smoking gun in my hand.

Isn't it funny how the moment you decide you want to continue living again is the same exact moment when it's gone forever? The universe has a funny way of showing its gratitude.

"I killed him," I whisper to the two older men standing in front of me, tears dripping onto the handcuffs that tightly wrap around my wrists. "I killed him!"

The metal bars slam shut as they thrust me inside a cold, dark cell, with nothing but a narrow bed and what resembled half a toilet bowl keeping me company. I turn around, screaming after the men as they begin to walk away.

"Wait! I... I can't stay here! I have to see him. I have to tell him I'm sorry!" I wrap my fingers around the metal bars, gripping with all the strength I could possibly muster, shaking it back and forth and screaming for the two men to come back.

"Should've thought of that before you shot him," one of them yells back from a distance, the echo bouncing off the walls.

Shot him. Yeah, I did that alright.

And now I'm facing life in prison.

A MONTH LATER, I receive a letter. It's from Ross.

> *Amber,*
>
> *I still haven't forgotten about that night. I thought you were different. And I actually really liked you. But then everything that happened with Dawson, the lies, the manipulation. I mean, what were you thinking? Putting a bullet through a man's head? To someone you used to love?*
>
> *Anyway, I just wanted to let you know that I still think about you from time to time, and*

part of me wants to come see you, but I know
that'll just end badly for the both of us.
I've actually started seeing Cindy recently. For
a ditzy cheerleader, she's actually kind of
smart, and a great kisser. But I guess that's
the least of your concerns.
I hope things get better for you. As much as
they can, anyway.
Ross

I grip the crumpled sheet of paper in between my hands and can feel my entire body shake. *Cindy.* The bane of my fucking existence. She ruined my life since the first day I stepped into the godforsaken school, and I swear. I swear, if I ever get out of here, she's the first one I'm coming after.

The End

Murder in Miami

Stalk the Author

Website:

https://www.kathrynreign.com/

Facebook Page:

https://www.facebook.com/authorkathrynreign

Instagram:

https://www.instagram.com/authorkathrynreign/

Goodreads:

https://www.goodreads.com/author/show/21854875.
Kathryn_Reign

BookBub:

https://www.bookbub.com/authors/kathryn-reign

Troubled Girls Find Love

9 781959 671503